A GOOD MAN COMES AROUND

ALSO BY HEATHER BLANTON

Grace Be a Lady

Hell-Bent on Blessings

A Scout for Skylar

Locket Full of Love

Carolina Homecoming

Romance in the Rockies Series

A Lady in Defiance

Hearts In Defiance

A Promise In Defiance

Daughter of Defiance

A Destiny in Defiance

Hope in Defiance

A Reckoning in Defiance

In Time For Christmas: A Novella

A GOOD MAN COMES AROUND

HEATHER BLANTON

A Good Man Comes Around
Paperback Edition

CKN Christian Publishing
An Imprint of Wolfpack Publishing
1707 E. Diana Street
Tampa, FL 33610

www.cknchristianpublishing.com

First edition published in 2020.

Paperback ISBN 979-8-89567-854-1 Ebook ISBN 979-8-89567-853-4

This book is dedicated to the hard-working authors of the Sweet Americana Sweethearts blog, who provide the world with sweet/clean historical romances about North Americans between 1820 and 1929.

A GOOD MAN COMES AROUND

PREFACE

Welcome to Jubilee Springs!

Jubilee Springs is a town of friendly folks in the Arkansas Valley of central Colorado that sprang up right after silver was discovered in the nearby hills. The western horizon is filled with vistas of the Rocky Mountains. Mount Shavano, at 14,000 feet in elevation, towers over other peaks. In the spring, melting snows reveal a shape that some call The Angel of Shavano.

If looking south, the Sangre de Cristo Mountains can be seen. The Arkansas River that runs through the valley provides plenty of irrigation for ranching and crops.

About three years ago, a pair of brothers took ownership of the largest mine in town. When grumblings about Jubilee Springs not having enough women reached their ears, the brothers, eager to keep their men happy and anchored to the community, took action. They contacted the Colorado Bridal Agency in Denver and set about bringing in mail-order brides for the employees.

While some men immediately took advantage of the idea, a few others needed substantial coaxing.

CHAPTER 1

Oliver Martin was old enough to know better. He lit the firecracker anyhow, enjoying the drunken glee sloshing through him. He glanced quickly over the batwings, tossed the sizzling noisemaker inside the busy Corner Saloon, then hunkered down to wait for the excitement.

His old friend John Fowler walked up, flicked his glance over the doors, and shook his head. His face, lined with fifty good years of hard living, darkened. "What have you done, Oliver?"

Tense with excitement, Oliver motioned with his eyes toward the saloon. "Just a little pop to wake 'em up."

John grabbed the top of the batwing and peered over it. His jaw tightened. Worried, Oliver stood up and tracked his friend's gaze. Because of the haze of cigar smoke, Oliver couldn't be sure, but he'd guess the firecracker went right underneath Jim Landers's feet. The gambler, known for his harsh methods of collecting debts, was holding a hand of cards, scrutinizing them with an icy stare.

A touch less whiskey and Oliver might have had cause to doubt the wisdom of this prank, but the liquor was chatting away, drowning out his good sense.

"Dang it, boy," John whispered. "You're not six, you're twenty-six. Act like a man."

The scolding was interrupted by a loud bang from right beneath Landers. The man yelped, his cards launched into the air, and he flipped over in his chair, his boots pointing straight at the ceiling.

The men playing poker leaped to their feet in confusion, and the whole saloon moved in one accord away from the sound. Bewildered rumblings quickly switched to grumbling as the other card players peeled Landers up off the floor. Cursing a shameful streak and shoving his comrades away, the gambler snatched at his cards scattered all around him—then his eyes met Oliver's over the batwings.

Even in Oliver's drunken state, he saw the rage boiling on the older man's chiseled face. "Uh oh." Why had he thought this was a good idea?

John sighed and pursed his lips. "Yep. Uh oh." His anger flared suddenly, surprising Oliver. "Run."

He and John turned and lunged for the boardwalk. It rocked beneath Oliver's feet, or so it seemed to him. The revolver strapped to his hip hampered his escape even more. Clearly, he shouldn't have finished off that bottle.

John grabbed his arm and dragged him forward. "He doesn't kill ya, I may well."

"I'm coming for you, Martin," Landers bellowed from the saloon's doorway. The man's heavy steps pounded after Oliver and he flinched. Of all the places that stupid firecracker could have landed, it had to blow up at the feet of one of the most ruthless men in town. The one man who couldn't take a joke.

Oliver and John ran down the crowded walk, ricocheting off people, earning grunts and curses. At River Road, John snatched Oliver back by the collar and pointed at a wagon. "Get in there." Oliver didn't argue. He scrambled up past a roll of barbed wire and slipped between two sacks of flour. An instant later, a canvas tarp landed on him. "Now, stay put," John ordered, "until either I come back for ya or you wake up on somebody's ranch." John's voice faded as he spoke. "I'm gettin' too old for this."

Was he hurrying off, leaving Oliver all alone? Oliver listened intently to the voices on the street. A group of men raging, cursing his name, came right up beside the wagon. He could hear them muttering, breathing threats.

"He's here somewhere."

Landers. Oliver clamped down on a gasp.

"And we'll find him. That shiftless no-account needs to be taught a lesson."

"That's right," someone agreed. "I'da won that hand if not for that firecracker."

"Well then, we can both stomp his head to mush."

Oliver broke out in a cold sweat listening to the promises of violence. *Good Lord, what was I thinking? I can't run a straight line, much less throw a punch. They'd beat the hound out of me.*

"That him?" Landers yelled. The angry, complaining mob moved off in a flurry of thudding, fading footfalls.

Time passed. Oliver wondered what John had done. Had he played the fox and led the hounds away? Stifling a yawn, he squirmed, shifting the .44 on his hip and settling more comfortably into the sack of flour. He wouldn't fall asleep. He would just wait. John would be back...

~

The wagon jolted and Oliver's eyes flew open. The tan-colored sky left him befuddled for a moment. Then it came back to him. The firecracker. Landers. He fought his way out from beneath the tarp and sat up. The shadows had lengthened, reaching all the way across the busy street now.

"See here," an indignant voice added to his confusion. "What are you doing in my wagon?" From the wagon seat, an old farmer sporting a long beard jabbed Oliver in the shoulder with an axe handle. "Get out. Get out."

Oliver scrambled away from the stick, cut his palm on the barbed wire, and nearly tripped coming out of the wagon, but righted himself on the street. The farmer dropped the axe handle and snapped the reins. Cringing against a blinding headache, Oliver wiped his hand on his pants and staggered off to his and John's cabin.

Unless he left Jubilee Springs, there was no way to avoid a beating from Landers. Maybe he should just go look for him now and get it over with. The idea had some appeal. Not much, though. No, Oliver decided he'd go home first. Have some coffee. Get this whiskey out of his system. Talk it over with John—

John? Where had he gone? Why hadn't he come back?

A little uneasy, Oliver picked up his pace, every footstep an icepick to his right eyeball. He was going to quit drinking.

Soon.

But first, get home.

He cut down an alley, skirted the Chinese laundry, and scrambled along the creek to his one-room cabin. The door was open, and he breathed a sigh of relief. John was here. Probably getting dinner started.

Only, John was not cooking. Oliver found him sitting at their rough-sawn plank table, a hunk of venison laid across one eye, a cup of coffee in his hand. A crimson smear crossed his face—from the bright-red swollen nose, Oliver guessed. His friend's knuckles were also scraped up, bloody, turning black-and-blue.

John looked up at Oliver, but his solemn expression didn't change.

Oliver swallowed. "Landers?"

John merely nodded.

Screwing his lips up tight, Oliver sat down opposite him. His self-loathing, an emotion he tried hard to ignore, roared to life. "Why didn't you just let them find me?"

John took a sip of his coffee. "I figured they'd just beat me. You...well, I figured they'd do worse."

"Am I square then with Landers?"

"Yep. You owe me, though. Twenty-five dollars. That's what he figures he lost on that hand of cards."

Oliver knew he was getting off light. Sighing heavily, he rubbed his scalp with all ten fingers, trying to massage away the headache. "You can't keep cleaning up my messes."

"Don't figure to." John set the cup down hard. "At least not anymore. I promised your pa I'd do what I could to turn you into a man. Reckon I've failed pretty miserably at that. Ever since that little filly jilted you, you've lost what sense you had."

Tired of this song and dance, Oliver rose and marched over to the stove. He didn't want a cup of coffee, but he poured one anyway. Slowly.

"You've got to settle down, son. Work this claim. There's gold out there—"

"Oh, don't give me that." Disgusted, Oliver spun. "Six months. Six months and we've barely panned enough out of this claim to keep a few groceries around."

John's eye narrowed. "You'll find gold, Oliver. Your ma saw it in a dream. And she was never wrong."

~

Butterflies cavorting in her stomach, Abigail Holt clutched her valise a little tighter and approached the train depot's station master. "Excuse me, could you direct me to the schoolhouse? I'm looking for Oliver Martin."

His expressionless face set like baked Georgia clay, the man pointed dully to his right and answered, "School's thatta way. End of town." Then he pushed his visor back an inch, revealing perhaps the slightest hint of curiosity. "You expect to see Oliver there, do you?"

"Where else would your schoolteacher be?"

"Schoolteacher."

He hadn't said it as if he questioned the label, nor did his bland expression change. No, it was the pause before the word that raised Abigail's suspicions and turned her butterflies to annoying gnats.

"Well..." The station master merely pointed to the right again. "End of town."

Abigail followed his pointing and strode toward Jubilee Springs' boardwalk. Around her, the Colorado mining town hummed and hustled. In the flow of the street, tin pans dinged and gonged as they rocked against saddles. Freight wagons, pack mules, miners, and businessmen bustled about, grumbling, fussing, moving, making use of every minute of daylight.

As she stepped up on the walk, a braying donkey and neighing horse battled for top volume at the hitching post. But they couldn't drown out the station master's rather enigmatic comments, which left her with the sense that something was askew. Before she found Mr. Martin, perhaps she should find the sheriff or a pastor. Someone who would give her an unvarnished appraisal of her potential groom. Miss Millard of the Colorado Bridal Agency had, of course, screened the man, and her reputation was stellar. *But...*

Abigail stopped. Something simply didn't feel right. The doubt had nagged her from the moment she had accepted Mr. Martin's proposal. Now it raged at her. What could be wrong? He *was* perfect. He'd met every one of her qualifications. Abigail had all but designed Mr. Martin from scratch.

Lean not to your own understanding...

The Scripture had been haunting her lately as well.

I don't expect him to be perfect, Lord. But certainly more respectable, kind, and clean than Sebastian was.

The letter she'd written to the wedding broker leaped up in her mind. She could recall it word-for-word: *I have been a widow now for almost a year. My sons, James and Artemus, are coming to ages where they need a father. I am in no mind to pursue a relationship for love. I want to pick out a husband the way an employer hires a new employee. The way one would evaluate an attorney or potential carpenter. I want to go about this logically and rationally and find the man best suited to raising my boys.*

I have a list of qualifications. Most importantly, my groom must abhor alcohol. I'll never live with a drunkard again. Next, he must be God-fearing, wise, slow to anger, thrifty with money, but not miserly. Neat in appearance and living conditions. Gainfully employed. He must have at least some education, not be given to foul language or card playing, and be a willing mentor to my sons.

*Lean not to your own understanding...*the gentle voice reminded her.

All right, all right, Lord, she fumed inwardly. *Maybe I did. Just a little. But please don't let that mean this is a disaster.*

Shooing the fear to the back of her mind, Abigail started a determined stride again. A few feet up, a man from the mercantile stepped out to sweep his entrance. His timing struck her as fortuitous and she determined to ask about this Mr. Martin one more time.

"Excuse me."

The man, tall, middle-aged, and soft-spoken, smiled pleasantly and paused his broom. "Yes, ma'am, what can I do for ya?"

"I'm looking for Mr. Oliver Martin. I understand he should be at the school."

This man did not hide his reaction. His eyebrows arched to the top of his forehead and he straightened up. "The school?"

His expression was answer enough. Abigail pulled her golden braid around and brushed her jaw with the end of it, a nervous habit. "I take it then that Mr. Martin is not the schoolteacher in Jubilee Springs?"

The storekeeper's brow dove in the opposite direction

and his expression darkened. He shifted the broom back and forth in his hands. "Ma'am, I fear I've stumbled into something that is none of my business."

"I understand." And she did. She also did not wish to put her humiliation on display here on the street. "Could you tell me—*would* you tell me—where I should look?"

The man took a deep breath and scratched his chin. "Well, it's pretty common knowledge he spends a lot of time at the saloon."

Abigail's spirits crashed through all the way to the earth's core. "The saloon." The man did not respond, merely nodded. The sympathy in his gentle, hazel eyes nearly worked a sob from her. Her thoughts roiling, Abigail wandered off.

She managed to walk several steps away from the mercantile before the knot in her throat worked a squeak from her. Desperate not to cry right here in the middle of the boardwalk, she shouldered her way over to the wall and turned her back to the traffic.

She'd spent all her money placing James and Artemus in a good boarding school back in Atlanta so she could make this trip and know they were taken care of. She had nothing left. If this Mr. Martin wouldn't pay her return ticket, what would she do? What would she do if she returned to Atlanta? A menial job? Multiple menial jobs, scraping by, always struggling for money?

Oh, stop it, Abigail. You're working yourself into a tizzy. Lord, I'm going to trust that things aren't as bleak as they're hinting. You're with me. It will be all right.

She lifted her chin, squared her shoulders, and trudged slowly down the walk. To find this Mr. Oliver Martin. And see just how bad her matrimonial situation was.

She noted out of the corner of her eye a man a few feet over, matching her dejected pace. Twenty-five or so, his shaggy, dark hair and wrinkled clothes framed a muscular build. He walked with his head down, hands shoved into his pockets, and was no more aware of her than a grazing horse swishing at flies. The aroma of whiskey drifted off him, and she wondered at a man drinking so early in the day.

They had walked past several more buildings when Abigail realized she had no idea where she was going. She stopped abruptly and placed the back of her hand on her forehead. She felt feverish, but wondered if she was imagining it.

"Ma'am, you all right?" The young man from beside her asked, dragging off his sweat-stained Stetson.

She shook her head. "I'm not sure. I'm looking for the saloon…unfortunately…"

"Ooh. I see," he said, as if he understood her meaning. Compassion softened his handsome, but scruffy face, and piercing blue eyes—perhaps a bit hazy with alcohol—did offer some compassion. "I'm on my way there…it's just up ahead."

Abigail gave a tiny gasp of horror at his skewed understanding. "No, it's not for me."

The young man tilted his head in question.

"I'm looking for someone. I was told he might be there."

"Oooh." He nodded again and half-smiled. As if in agreement, they both started walking, though at a slower pace. "What's his name?" he asked cheerfully. "Maybe I know him. I drink with—I mean, I know about everybody in Jubilee."

"Oliver Martin."

Her companion stopped as suddenly as if manacles had been slapped on his feet. Clenching his jaw, he slowly slid his gaze over to Abigail. He surveyed her, top to bottom, pausing briefly on her suitcase. She had the impression that whatever alcohol might be in his system had suddenly evaporated and left him stone-cold sober. "What do you want with him?"

Normally, she would not have confided such information to a stranger, but the heat in his eyes, it raised goosebumps on her arms. The air seemed to crackle with electricity. "I was supposed to be his bride."

Her companion stopped as suddenly as if manacles had been slapped on his feet. Clenching his jaw, he slowly slid his gaze over to Abigail. He surveyed her, top to bottom, pausing briefly on her suitcase. She had the impression that whatever alcohol might be in his system had suddenly evaporated and left him stone-cold sober. "What do you want with him?"

Normally, she would not have confided such information to a stranger, but the heat in his eyes raised goosebumps on her arms. The air seemed to crackle with electricity. "I was supposed to be his bride."

CHAPTER 2

Dread coursed through Abigail, and her body felt as if it were melting. She'd come all this way to meet disaster. "You're Mr. Martin, aren't you?"

The man slapped a hand over his mouth, looked one way then another—as if he wanted to run for a drink—then finally stepped over and leaned his back against the wall of the gun shop. Head hanging, shoulders slumped, he let out what sounded like a disgusted sigh and replaced his hat. He was a picture of agony.

Abigail swallowed some rising nausea and crossed the boardwalk to join him, her valise clutched in front of her like a shield. She caught a whiff of gun oil, mingled with the scent of the whiskey and a decidedly unpleasant body odor. *What a waste. A young, handsome man going to seed.*

Absently, Mr. Martin picked his hat up, ran his hands through his unkempt brown hair, and dropped it back in place. "John. John did this." He kicked the wall. "I knew he was up to something."

"Are you saying you don't have any knowledge of me?

You didn't answer an ad for a bride?" Panic crept into her voice. "You're not looking for a wife?"

"No. I mean, yes." He flinched. "I mean, I am not looking for a wife. I sure as heck didn't send off for one. You sound like you're a long way from home."

"Atlanta." She nearly spat the word at him. She huffed a breath, grasping for some self-control. "And this leaves me in a fine mess." Layers of disappointment piled up in Abigail, heavy and thick, but anger slowly spread over them all like the icing on a cake. She would not stand here wallowing in despair. She would not let yet another man make her life miserable. "I don't know who this John is, but I have a letter and a matrimonial contract that he"—she let her eyes roam over his bedraggled appearance—"or you—one of you—has clearly violated. I don't see how you fit any of my requested qualifications."

Mr. Martin snapped to and crossed his arms over his chest, but there was a slight sway in his stance. "Hey now—"

"I've been brought here under false pretenses. Someone is going to pay to send me home *and* for my trouble in coming here." Heedless of the rising volume of her voice, she waved a finger in Mr. Martin's face. "I left my two children in a respectable, *expensive* boarding school to travel halfway across the country to marry you. You said you would pay to bring them out here in a few months. Can you even grasp the turmoil and heartache you are causing—"

"Whoa, whoa," Mr. Martin patted the air. "Quit shoutin'."

"You're early, ma'am."

She and Mr. Martin turned at the slow, easy drawl. An

older man, in his fifties, with long, salt-and-pepper hair touching his shoulders, ambled up. Wrinkles at the corners of his merry blue eyes and the rebellious twitch on his lips betrayed his amusement as he surveyed Abigail. "You must be Mrs. Holt." He extended his hand.

Mr. Martin stepped between them and thumped the man on the chest. "What have you done, John? Tell me you didn't go and get me a bride like all those blockheads did for the Fourth of July." He sounded utterly horrified at the idea, and Abigail fought against taking his displeasure personally. He was no prize himself.

"That is exactly what gave me the idea. And look at her." He stepped away from Mr. Martin and gestured grandly at Abigail. "She's a beautiful Southern belle with a voice that drips magnolias and moonlight. She's the prettiest mail-order bride this town has seen yet."

"That's got nothing to do with it." Mr. Martin's face flushed. "You're crazy. I'm not taking a wife. What made you go and do such a foolish thing? Especially without telling me."

His friend chuckled. "Maybe I had a little too much whiskey one evening." He winked at Abigail. "Or maybe I figured the only way to settle this fool down was to find him the right wife."

Abigail would not be swayed by a roguish demeanor. "Mr....?"

"Fowler." He offered his hand. "John Fowler."

The two shook, but Abigail was not mollified. "Mr. Fowler, I am not amused, to say the least. In fact, I am very angry. You have lied to me and used me. You've pulled me away from the two things in this world that matter—" Unexpectedly, her voice broke and a knot formed in her throat. "That matter most to me—my children. Now you will pay for me to go home, and I demand compensation for my trouble. In fact"—she scrambled quickly inside her valise, remembering the contract—"you have violated the terms of our contract on several issues." She pulled an envelope out and waved it at them. "Therefore, you have to pay remuneration of two hundred dollars for the malfeasance."

Both men's eyes widened to the size of full moons. Then Mr. Fowler's face darkened and his good humor faded. "What are you talking about?" He snatched the envelope from her and pulled out the contract. Abigail waited while the two men scanned the document.

After a moment, Mr. Fowler folded the paper and slipped it back into the envelope. "Well, I guess we'll have to pay."

"We don't have two—"

Mr. Fowler smacked Mr. Martin hard in the stomach, cutting him off. "But, the first thing we should do, Mrs. Holt, is get you off the street. Mr. Martin here will pay to put you up in the hotel for a few days while we sort this out."

"Me? Why do I have to pay? I didn't bring her here."

"No, but you're—!" Mr. Fowler clamped down on his burst of anger and tried again. "You're taking the lady's valise and walking her on over to the inn. Does that meet with your approval, ma'am?"

"If I refuse, I will find myself out on the street. Since you did bring me here under false pretenses, I feel decent lodgings is the least you can do."

"Yes, ma'am." Mr. Fowler turned to Mr. Martin. "Meet me back at the cabin once she's settled."

Quivering with what Abigail assumed was barely controlled rage, Mr. Martin grabbed her valise, but she resisted. Their eyes locked. After a moment, they both huffed with resignation, and she released her bag to him. "I also have a trunk."

"I'll get that handled for you, Mrs. Holt," Mr. Fowler offered, walking away.

Mr. Martin glared at his friend, as if hoping he might get run over by a freight wagon.

Oliver wasn't fit to be tied over this ridiculous situation. He was on the verge of a flat-out apoplectic fit. He couldn't bring himself to look at Mrs. Holt as they marched down the boardwalk. He was so angry. With John. With her and her snooty attitude. But mostly with John. His old friend had a beating coming over this. He'd interfered with Oliver's life one time too many.

"Why would he do this?" Mrs. Holt asked, absently watching the busy street. "Does he make a practice of lying and manipulating people?"

Oliver had to admit he liked hearing her talk, the way she drew out her long *i's,* but the question showed her ignorance of John. "He's my best friend and he's a good man." His defense, however, in light of the situation, sounded foolish. He sighed. "He thought he was doing a good thing, I'm sure. He should have talked to me first, though." The explanation seemed to soften Mrs. Holt. For some reason, that made some of Oliver's anger slip away. "We've been friends a long time. I grew up around John. He promised my pa he'd take care of me if anything ever happened—" He dropped it there.

She didn't need all the details. "He cares about you then. Something to be said for that."

If she only knew. Oliver rubbed his neck, trying to get the ins and outs of this mess settled in his mind. But something stuck in his craw. "Why don't I meet any of your qualifications? You don't even know me."

"You drink, obviously."

"Some. Yes."

"Therefore, you're probably not very fiscally responsible."

"Fiscally resp—?"

"Are you good with managing your money? When you're not drinking it."

Oliver tugged at his frayed collar. "Well, things are a little tight right now—"

"Are you gainfully employed?"

"We have a gold stake down by the river." He heard the lack of confidence in his own voice.

"Do you curse?"

"Every now and then."

"Do you keep company with sporting women?"

"No." *Well, there was that one time with Marlene...*

"I asked that my potential groom be neat in appearance and living conditions. Based on your smell, I would assume your cabin is no cleaner than you are."

Oliver clamped his jaw tight. The woman could slice a man with that tongue as easily as a butcher could cut out a sirloin. There was no way this would have ever worked. "Is that all?"

"No, there were a few others, but why bother explaining them?"

They walked the last few feet in silence, then entered the hotel. Oliver registered Mrs. Holt, to the curious look of young Jude Debenham, the inn's owner, and escorted her to her room. Slipping the key into the door, he wondered about her requirements for sainthood. "That list was awfully precise. You reckon any man can be that perfect?"

"It is not a list for a perfect man, merely a good man. I had the opposite for too long."

Oliver saw the shadow of anger, maybe regret, cross her face. She *was* beautiful. He liked her little, upturned nose, glittering, green eyes, and shiny gold hair. She had some inviting curves, too. But that tongue. It would take a special man to survive it. "What happened to your first husband?"

"Drank himself to death."

He nodded, wondering if she'd driven him to it. He regretted the thought. All joking aside, he'd seen more than one man drown in whiskey. Blaming it on the woman was pretty pathetic. Men made their own choices.

The hypocrisy of the observation slapped him in the face.

His anger surging again, this time at himself, he opened the door for her and stepped back. "Well, Mrs. Holt, I reckon John'll be in touch."

"Thank you, Mr. Martin."

He hesitated for a moment, unsure why he was dallying. But when she touched the back of her fingers to her nose, subtly veiling her distaste with his smell, he took the hint and departed without another word…

Wishing he was headed for the saloon.

~

Oliver had never wanted to punch John Fowler so bad in over twenty years of their acquaintance. He stormed into the dark cabin, flipped a chair out of his way, and marched up to John, who was standing at the stove, nonchalantly frying a steak.

"I ought to clean your clock, old man."

"I suppose you could try." John flipped the steak but didn't look up. "Stand a better chance if you sober up first," he muttered.

Oliver tossed his hat off into a corner and paced around the dank, musty-smelling cabin. Frustration oozed from him and he kicked a pile of dirty clothes out of his way. "Why would you do this? You had no right to meddle and create a mess like this."

"I was tired of getting beat up for you."

Oliver rolled his eyes to the ceiling. John had a point. He'd been through the mill and back again for an old comrade's son. Still…Oliver turned just as John was settling at the table and reaching for the salt.

"I've done some dumb things, true. And you've paid for 'em a time or two, but this…this is crazy."

"Maybe."

John seemed oblivious to the mess, and that riled Oliver even more. "How many times have I told you I'm done with women? They're all liars. And this one—oh, this one has a mouth on her that can dice a man like you do potatoes."

John chuckled, as if the image tickled him, and sliced into his steak.

"And you—" Oliver marched over to the table. "Did you even bother to read her ad? She has a list of qualifications Jesus wouldn't meet."

John frowned, rolled the bite of steak around in his mouth like he was contemplating the observation, but then reached for the salt shaker again.

Exasperated, Oliver threw up his hands. "Little Miss High-and-Mighty would never consider somebody like me, John. This whole thing is what Pa would have called a stick in the wheel." Oliver's temper snapped. "And it's all your fault."

John's gaze flicked up. The cold, hard look hit Oliver hard and he backed up a step.

"Boy," John waved a fork at him, "You have been runnin' on the stupid side of wild for too long. Somethin' had to give. Now I stepped outta line bringing that little filly here, maybe. Maybe not. It's turning into a royal misunderstanding for sure, but I think you need to give her a chance."

Oliver couldn't believe what he was hearing. "You're out of your mind. Plumb loco. Even if I was thinking about this blockhead idea of yours, where would she stay?" John raised his eyebrows. Oliver gulped. "I mean, where would you stay?"

"I'd stay in the barn, and you could add a room onto this hovel."

Oliver snorted and hung his head. "We can barely afford to feed ourselves. How was I supposed to take care of a wife?"

"I figured you'd find a way. But back off on your

drinkin'. Work that claim out there more than a few hours a day and you'd pull some gold out of the mud."

"Yeah, that's what I wanna do the rest of my life. Play in the mud."

"What *do* you want to do the rest of your life?"

Oliver stared at his friend, who stared back, hard. Waiting.

He shrugged. "I don't know."

"A woman can help a man figure out questions like that."

Oliver shook his head and sat down at the table. The *I-don't-know* answer had reminded him again that he was bogged down. Like a wagon stuck in deep, muddy ruts. Avonia leaving him at the altar that way had just sort of wrung the desire for anything more right out of him. *Men make their own choices...*the thought echoed accusingly in his head.

"You should give her a chance. She seems like a nice gal."

Oliver gave a derisive snort. "They all do at first."

Abigail sat down on the bed, still clutching her valise. The room, filling now with long shadows, was plain, offering only a bed, a worn rug, and a dresser. A pitcher and wash-basin sat on the marble top, a fresh towel folded beside them. She poured some water and splashed her face. The cool felt good, but unexpectedly, a sob escaped her, and she allowed herself a moment to cry.

No, it wouldn't change anything or help the situation, but it had been so long since she'd cried about anything.

She missed her boys. She was out of money. This mail-order bride idea had been a desperate gamble that was ending in disaster.

And this whining isn't helping. Oh, Lord, what am I going to do?

Abigail splashed her face again, wiped away the tears, and dried off. The room didn't even have a mirror. She must look a sight but had no way to fix that either. More worrisome, she was hungry, but didn't have enough money for a meal. Perhaps she could find the mercantile and at least buy an apple—

Someone knocked at the door and Abigail jumped, her hand flying to her throat. "Yes?"

"Ma'am, I have your dinner."

Dinner? "I didn't order—"

"Yes, ma'am, Oliver ordered it for you before he left."

Well, maybe the man had one or two redeeming qualities after all.

Her spirits buoyed by the blessing of a meal, Abigail savored the country-fried steak, applesauce, and pinto beans like no other dinner she'd ever had. In fact, she said grace over the food with a true heart of gratitude.

Afterward, she lay down on the bed to pray, curling up into a little ball. She pondered the meal again. How many times had she eaten with her boys these last several months, said the blessing over the food, but hadn't heard or felt the words? At least coming to Jubilee Springs had put her in mind to be thankful for her blessings, appreciate the moments with her children, and be more grateful to her Lord.

"Thank you, Father," she whispered. "Thank You that even though I'm not with my boys, this marriage idea seems to have been a disaster, and I am broke...I feel Your presence stronger than I have in a long time. And I know You'll help me find and take the next step."

Somewhere along the line, praying gave way to exhaustion and Abigail drifted into a peaceful sleep. She awoke the next morning rested and unexpectedly optimistic. She had a Scripture echoing in her mind as well.

Whatever you do, work at it with all your heart, as working for the Lord, not for human masters.

Stretching, she pondered the Word. *I don't know to what I should apply that to, Lord, but I'm eager for You to show me.*

Wishing Mr. Martin would have supplied breakfast, too, she dug through her trunk and slipped into a light-blue cotton day dress. To forget her hunger, she headed out to explore the bustling mining town of Jubilee Springs. Besides, she couldn't stand the thought of sitting around doing nothing while Mr. Martin and Mr. Fowler argued about whose responsibility she was. Some fresh air and a tour of the town might help her clear her head and form a plan.

She exited the River Valley Inn and turned right on Telegraph Street, heading away from the train depot. Again, the hustle-and-bustle of the town impressed her. The sound of pounding hammers and rhythmic saws provided a melody for the activity. Horses neighed and dogs barked. Men's voices fought to rise above the activity. Miners, cowboys, and gentlemen nodded appreciatively at Abigail. She responded stiffly, intent on sending the correct message, nothing inviting.

A man in a black apron hurried past her, leaving a familiar scent in his wake. She slowed her pace. The smell reminded her of—

India ink?

Curious, she followed him as he skirted and sidestepped traffic on the boardwalk. The scent brought back pleasant memories of her father's print shop. Abigail had become quite good at running his press before his passing, but she had a special gift for typesetting. She had such a knack for laying out copy backward that her father had been contemplating starting a newspaper.

And then Sebastian had entered the picture and Abigail had fallen hopelessly—foolishly—in love. With a drunk. Oh, an attorney with accolades, but a drunk, nonetheless. Not a fairy-tale ending.

Finally, two buildings down, the man turned and disappeared into a shop. Abigail approached the door slowly and inhaled the familiar, comforting smells of ink and paper. Yearning for a little peace, she pushed open the door. The bell overhead rang out, announcing her entrance.

The man had just stepped behind the counter and was retying his apron. He looked up at the sound of potential business. Tall, gangly, nearing sixty or so, he smiled warmly and pushed his spectacles up on his nose. "Mornin', ma'am. Can I help you with your printing needs today? Wait—" He held up a bony finger. "Wedding invitations?"

Abigail unintentionally flinched. The man's lined face softened to sympathy. "I'm sorry. Gettin' ahead of myself. Um…" He stepped around the counter and met Abigail in the middle of the shop floor. "I'm Clem Stewart. This is my shop. Is there something I can do for ya?"

"Honestly, Mr. Stewart..." Abigail glanced around the room, cluttered with shelves of messily stacked paper, an antique flatbed printing press, boxes scattered about, and the counter buried in what appeared to be orders ready for pick up. "My father used to own a print shop. I just miss the smells of...better days, you could say."

"Doin' a little reminiscing, are you?" He pursed his lips in a kind gesture. "You're new in town, aren't you?"

Nodding, Abigail drifted over to the press. "Yes." She ran her hand lightly across the old machine. "My father had one very similar to this. I believe his was a Franklin."

"Good press. I have a newer Washington in the back. It's replacing that piece of junk."

"Oh, this isn't a terrible machine. It just has to be handled gently and used for short runs."

Mr. Stewart's eyes glinted with interest. "What did you do in your father's shop? Exactly?"

"Oh, wedding invitations, business cards, and then eventually longer pamphlets because I can typeset." She picked up the press's handle, a long piece of threaded iron called the Devil's Tail, inserted it in the press's head, and began screwing it into place.

"You can typeset? That's not a skill that comes easily to most people."

Abigail couldn't help but smile. "Yes, typesetters were the bane of my father's business until we discovered I had a proclivity for the task. Apparently, I think backward as easily as I think forward."

Mr. Stewart folded his arms and began stroking his chin. "I find myself commiserating with your father on that very aspect. Your accent. You're from the South somewhere?"

"Yes, sir. Atlanta."

"Will you be staying in Jubilee Springs?"

Abigail worked the handle back and forth. It felt good to have her hands on the Devil's Tail. She only wished she could tie a knot in it, he'd been bringing her so much misery these last few years. But to the man's question... "I'm not quite sure what my plans are."

Mr. Stewart moseyed on back behind the counter and sat down on a stool, still rubbing his chin. "I have been without a decent typesetter for months now. I'm having to do all the work myself, which is slowing down my production. If I had a cracker-jack typesetter—gee, I could boost my turn-out by a good twenty-five percent or more." He tilted his head and studied Abigail. "More. You aren't looking for a job, are you?"

Abigail sucked in a breath that sounded like a blacksmith's bellows. "You need a typesetter?" *Lord, would You make it this simple and clear?*

Whatever you do, work at it with all your heart, as working for the Lord...

"I'd want you to prove yourself, of course. Not that I'm doubting your word, but seein' as how I don't really know you—"

"Of course. I wouldn't mind. But..." she trailed off. Did she want a job? This was a new town. It would mean a fresh start. A chance to be in control of her own destiny for once, without a man to prop her up. But what of the boys? They still needed a father.

"Well, I can see you need to think about it." He slapped the counter lightly. "Will you, though? Think about it, Miss—sorry, I never even got your name."

"Abigail Holt."

"Well, Miss Holt, you'll consider it? I'll pay you what I'd pay a man."

"I will consider it, Mr. Stewart. Seriously."

~

"I will consider it, Mr. Stewart. Seriously."

Very seriously indeed. Abigail wandered around Jubilee Springs for another few hours, getting the lay of the land, so to speak. But she kept going back to the conversation with Mr. Stewart. The offer of a job was amazingly fortuitous.

And that is exactly how You work, Father. You have promised to take care of me, and You haven't let me down yet.

Her steps lightened the more she walked. She could do this. She could get a job as a typesetter. In no time, she'd have the money to bring James and Artemus west to join her. A passing cowboy tipped his hat out of politeness. The town was friendly, safe, and growing. A good place to raise children. *This* felt right.

And a father for the boys might come along.

The thought brought her back to earth. No, she did not need a husband. She did not need a man in her life. But her children needed a father. Was there someone in this town who could match up to her list?

"Mrs. Holt," a voice hailed from behind her. She spun and saw Mr. Fowler jogging down the boardwalk toward her. "I have looked everywhere for you today. I kept missing you by mere minutes."

"Well, now you have found me, Mr. Fowler. What can I do for you?"

"Thought I might buy you lunch, if you're hungry."

She was tempted to say no out of pure pride, but her stomach growled. She swallowed against the grumbling. "I could eat."

~

Mr. Fowler handed the menu to a slight man of Hispanic heritage and turned back to Abigail. "As I was saying, we don't have the whole two hundred here, but if you're set on going home, we'll get it."

"But...?" Abigail prodded, leaning back in her café seat. She sensed there was more.

"But I—we—I mean, *we* think you should give Jubilee Springs a chance. Try the town on for size. Maybe you'll want to stay, and maybe you'll find that Oliver could be to your liking."

"Mr. Fowler, I don't mean to offend, but you lied to me in every possible way regarding Mr. Martin. To your credit —and to his character, I suppose—I think you did this because you believe in him. But it was wrong. As I've said, you have separated me from my children, and I am having difficulty getting past that."

"Yes, ma'am." He chewed on his cheek and stared down at the red-checked tablecloth, drumming his fingers. For the first time, Abigail noted he was missing his ring finger.

"I did take some pretty tall liberties with this situation," he conceded. "And I'm sorry. If it's any consolation, I believe you're the perfect woman for Oliver."

Her mouth fell open. "How can you say that? You don't even know me."

He sucked in a deep breath, let it slip out slowly, thoughtfully. "I'm a God-fearin' man and I just know...I *know* there's a plan here. And in my defense, I didn't exactly lie. At one time in his life, Oliver was all those things you listed in your letter. Once upon a time. I thought maybe you'd help him find himself again."

The older man's gentle honesty and vulnerability touched Abigail. She'd never had a friend like this in her life. Other than her father. He'd believed in her, wanted the best for her. Had ardently been against her marriage to Sebastian.

She shook her head, recoiling at going down that rabbit trail. "Were you married? I see your ring finger is missing."

Chuckling, Mr. Fowler raised his hand and stared at the empty space. But Abigail thought he was seeing something more.

"I understand it is a common injury to men who wear their wedding rings during work hours."

"Yep. It is." He flexed his fingers. "Had a wife who caught me cheating, and she was dangerous with a knife. 'Bout lost the fingers on either side of it." He *tsked* at the memory. "I always figured I was kinda lucky, though. She could have gone after something more important than my fingers."

At first, Abigail was appalled at his crude humor, but laughter burst forth, despite her attempt at maintaining some propriety. Embarrassment flushed her cheeks. "I'm sorry, I shouldn't laugh."

"Why not? It's funny now. It weren't then. But now it is."

In spite of his rough edges, Abigail found herself drawn to John Fowler. And curious about Oliver Martin. "What happened to Mr. Martin? What changed him?"

"Avonia Harper. A bird brain if ever there was one, but

pretty as the day is long. And she could talk. Oh, my how that young gal could sweet-talk a man into a real pretzel knot. Or any shape she cared to. Anyhow, Oliver's so gun-shy now, he won't look at another woman. Not for anything real anyway. He didn't like getting hurt."

"No one does."

"True. But sometimes there is a purpose for the pain."

She could agree with that. Thanks to Sebastian, she would never again marry a drinking man. And like Mr. Martin, she too was tired of love's ability to exact excruciating pain. Maybe they were both better off avoiding romantic entanglements for the rest of their lives. The idea was tempting.

"Oliver likes you. I can tell. You're the first woman since Avonia that he's gotten so fired up about."

"I would credit the situation for that."

"Not me. I know him better."

"How is it that you are so responsible for him? He's a grown man."

"His pa was my best friend, and he asked me to watch over Oliver if something ever happened. Somethin' did. Oliver is a fine young man, and he was doin' real well there for a while. Didn't need me at all…until Avonia."

"What did she do to him?"

"One day they're planning their wedding, the next she's run off with some actor. Last I heard, she was performing Shakespeare up in Cheyenne."

A waitress interrupted them, delivering plates of fried chicken, mashed potatoes, cheese biscuits, and glazed carrots. Abigail and Mr. Fowler offered silent blessings and dove in. The conversation hit a lull until a good percentage of the food had vanished. But she suspected they were both planning the rest of the conversation. She certainly was.

"I take it from this conversation, you do not have two hundred dollars to send me back to Atlanta."

Mr. Fowler paused, a coffee cup at his lips, he set it back down on the table. "No, ma'am, we can get it pretty darn quick and you can leave tomorrow if that's your choice. But I wonder what you're going back to." He paused. "Jubilee Springs is a nice town with nice folks. Nice businesses. You could probably get decent work. Something fit for a nice gal. Waiting on tables. Cleaning rooms—"

"Setting type at the print shop?"

She hadn't meant to say that out loud, but Mr. Fowler's eyebrow twitched up. "Yeah, setting type at the print shop."

"Setting type," she repeated softly. She ran her finger along the rim of her water glass. "How much time do I have? I mean, how long before you need me to get out of the hotel?"

"I figure we can put you up for two weeks."

"And at any moment, if I decide to go back to Atlanta…?"

"I'll buy the ticket *plus* give you the cash. I'll just need a day or two to get it wired to the bank."

"Then, Mr. Fowler, I believe I will give Jubilee Springs a chance to convince me of its benefits."

CHAPTER 3

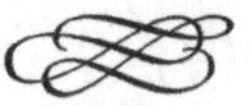

Oliver was tired of being wet and cold. Bent over, he sloshed the pan of icy water around and around for the millionth time today. A couple of yellow flakes sparkled in the swishing gravel. Slowly, he poured off most of the water and plucked out the shiny pieces of gold, depositing them in the leather pouch hanging at his waist. Pushing an index finger around in the remaining pebbles and sand, he discovered one tiny nugget, about an eighth the size of his pinky fingernail.

"Hmmm," he grunted, halfway pleased. The last two days, he'd actually pulled some gold out of their claim. Maybe things were looking up, but he wouldn't let his hopes rise…yet. He straightened and groaned over his tight back.

"Got something?" John asked from the back porch of the cabin.

Oliver eyed the gold in the palm of his hand. "A little more than yesterday. Maybe we're hitting a streak." He dipped the pan back in the water to rinse it out, then cast it to the shore as he strode out. He couldn't feel his toes. "I'm gonna clean up a little and go have breakfast in town." He tramped up the steps and handed John the pouch with the gold. "Here ya go, partner."

He started to push the back door open, but froze when John asked, "You goin' to check on Mrs. Holt?"

"Why would I do that?"

"I told you I told her we'd put her up for a couple of weeks at the inn. It's been a few days. One of us ought to go see if she's made any plans yet."

Oliver *had* toyed with the idea of getting breakfast at the inn. He drummed his fingers on the doorknob. "Yeah, all right. Maybe she'll tell me she's getting a job and we can be done worrying about her."

"You been worrying about her?"

"What?"

"You just said maybe if she gets a job we can be done worrying about her."

Anger flamed in Oliver like kerosene poured on an open fire. "I'm not worrying about *her*. I'm worrying about coming up with two hundred dollars to ship her back to Atlanta."

"If you say so."

Oliver was tempted to argue but decided retreat might be safer.

~

Abigail wouldn't have thought getting a job could spawn such immense satisfaction. Grinning, she stepped outside the print shop and inhaled the scent of summer's morning dew, along with the odor of horses and fresh-cut lumber. At this hour, the town was beginning to stretch and yawn and prepare for a new day. Watching it wake up was a pleasant distraction.

She fanned the stack of handbills she'd typeset herself and lifted her chin with pride. Handbills announcing Jubilee's first newspaper and its advertising rates. She was a salesperson *and* the typesetter. Surely it would not be long before she had the funds to send for her boys. Her face almost hurt from the huge grin she was wearing.

Her expression garnered a curious look from a miner bouncing by on an old, tattered mule. Yes, Abigail *was* grinning like a fool, but for the first time in months, she had something to grin about. A job. Hope that her future might be brighter than she had anticipated. She would have her boys with her before fall. She wasn't trapped in yet another loveless marriage. She couldn't be happier that things had fallen through with Mr. Martin.

In fact, Abigail wanted to spread her arms and spin around like a twirling toddler.

Oh, Lord, I can't ask for much more. Thank You.

Of course, her children still needed a father, but now Abigail had *time*. Time to look. Time to pray about the right man. She wouldn't get ahead of God again.

I won't lean on my own understanding, Lord. I promise. And I know You'll bring me the right man at the right time.

Letting go of that particular issue, she tugged on her shirtwaist, fluffed the lace on her bustle, and hurried down the walk, intent on letting every business in Jubilee Springs know about the newspaper. Mr. Stewart had agreed to pay her for typesetting as well as any advertising she could muster up. She meant to make every barber shop, apothecary shop, leather shop, and any other shop aware of the forthcoming publication.

The woman at the apothecary shop was excited about the potential opportunity to advertise the personal benefits of her medicinal inventory. The owner of the leather shop wasn't interested until Abigail pointed out that a newspaper advertisement would be a fine way to notify customers that their orders were ready, as well as sell any inventory for which customers never returned.

The town barber proved a stiffer challenge. He wasn't convinced of the need for advertising, seeing as how he had no competition in Jubilee Springs, though Abigail warned competition would invariably come. The gentleman said he would worry about the inevitable when it happened.

Undaunted by the one rejection, she left his shop and turned left, walking slowly. From her reticule, she pulled out the map Mr. Debenham from the inn had sketched for her and studied the town.

Where to next?

The bakery was at the end of the street ahead, or if she turned back and walked in the opposite direction, she could stop in at the butcher shop. Or perhaps she should visit the businesses a few streets out and work her way back?

She did want to stop in at the Corner Saloon and Billiard Parlor on Telegraph Street. In her experience with her father's print shop, these businesses advertised a fair amount. They had often ordered handbills promoting a new singer, some traveling troupe of actors, even high-stakes card tournaments. Why should the saloon here in Jubilee Springs be any different? Besides, the saloon did have competition and needed to distinguish itself from the one that offered *upstairs girls.* Resolute, Abigail marched onward to the business.

The Corner Saloon was obviously called such because of its corner entrance that straddled both Telegraph Street and River Road. Abigail stepped into its shadowy doorway and peered over the batwings. A gray haze hung above the felt-topped tables, fogging the milling, moving bodies. A less-than-gifted pianist eagerly hammered out "The Battle Hymn of the Republic." The raucous music almost drowned out voices raised in song.

"...He is trampling out the vineyards where the grapes of wrath are stored," a chorus of drunken voices bellowed. Quite the exuberant crowd for the hour. Men who should be home with their wives and families.

Should *she* even be here?

Before Abigail could decide, she felt a hard slap to her bottom, albeit one muffled by her large bustle.

"Hey, sugar, you lookin' for work?"

Abigail gasped and spun on the stranger. A man with stringy hair, a long face, bulging, bloodshot eyes, and big, crooked teeth leered at her.

The stranger's unruly behavior outraged Abigail as indignation colored her cheeks. "I beg your pardon."

"You're at the wrong saloon, sister." The man snaked his hand around her waist. "You want the Silver Dollar over near the mine. I'll show ya."

Sputtering in shock and grimacing at the man's body odor, Abigail knocked his hand off her waist and stepped back. "H-how dare you. I am not looking for employment, you—you"—she scanned his filthy, unkempt frame—"you slovenly, odiferous drunkard."

His brow dove and his face lost its good humor. "You got a mouth on you, girl, that could sure be put to better use."

"All right, that's enough, Wilkins."

In spite of herself, Abigail was relieved to hear a familiar voice.

Mr. Martin ambled up the boardwalk. "Take your foul mouth inside and leave the lady alone."

Wilkins glared. "Oliver, you ain't won a fight in this town since you got here, including with me. Don't make me whup you again in front of the *lady*." He emphasized the last word as if it was delightfully entertaining. "Now run along before you embarrass yourself."

Mr. Martin regarded Wilkins with a solemn expression. Abigail would not have classified the dark look as thoughtful. Rather, she would have labeled it resignation.

"Did you touch her?"

"What?"

Mr. Martin sighed, an exasperated sound. He looked at Abigail. "Did he touch you?"

"Yes, he slapped my—I mean, yes." Mortified, she didn't wish to say more.

He shifted back to Wilkins. "Apologize to her."

"What?" The man shook his head as if he couldn't believe his ears.

"Apologize to her for your rude behavior."

Wilkins turned his head like a puppy discovering a new sound. "You drinking already today?"

"Unfortunately, no. I am heading to the inn for some eggs and bacon. I'd like to get there before they're all gone. But first I have to hear you tell Mrs. Holt that you mean her no harm and that you are sorry for embarrassing her."

Wilkins scratched his ear. "What are you gonna do about it, if I don't?"

"What am I gonna do about it?" There in front of the odd-shaped entrance to the Corner Saloon, Mr. Martin raised his chin, as if resolving something in his mind. "What I should have done the first time we tangled. Kick your—" The profanity was lost in a blur of motion.

Mr. Martin drew back and punched Wilkins square in the nose, so hard and fast that if Abigail had blinked, she would have missed it. Blood gushed. She squealed. Wilkins hollered and clutched his face, moaning and bewailing the attack.

Mr. Martin drew himself up to his full height and raised his fist again. "You can't treat a lady that way and not expect to suffer some harm."

"You broke my nose," the man cried through gushing blood.

"Get out of here or I'll break something else."

Attempting to singe Mr. Martin with a baleful glare, Mr. Wilkins yanked a bandana from his pocket, crushed it to his face, and staggered off. "I like you better drunk." His voice now had a muffled, nasally quality. "You're not friendly sober. Not at all."

Abigail watched the ruffian for a moment, but quickly snapped her gaze back to Mr. Martin. He stood with his shoulders straight, chin up, ice-blue eyes trained intently on the departing man. In her estimation, this almost-groom seemed taller, stronger somehow. She realized she was clutching the handbills in front of her bosom like a frightened child and lowered them.

The movement brought him back around to her. "What are you doing?" He sounded annoyed, which in turn annoyed and puzzled her. "Here," he added. "What are you doing here? Lookin' for me?"

"I was looking for the owner. Believe it or not, my every waking moment in Jubilee Springs has not been focused on resolving our disastrous arrangement."

He scowled, raised his cowboy hat, shook his hair, then deposited the cap back in place. "I didn't mean to imply that. But I couldn't figure any other reason for you being here."

His assumption made sense and Abigail tamped down her anger. After all, the man had just rescued her. However, he had resorted to violence so quickly. She glanced down the boardwalk one last time. "Thank you for intervening." She almost admired him for it, but his willingness to fight also showed a potential hair-trigger. "I have to ask, was it necessary to strike him?"

Mr. Martin turned to face her and cocked his head a little, openly studying her. "Wondering if my temper is another disqualification?"

"About that. Actually, Mr. Martin, we should talk."

"Why I came here today. After breakfast, I was gonna come find you."

Then why was he near the saloon? How many times had she and the boys come *after* a beer or two…or twenty?

Her fond memories of life with a drunkard must have shown on her face. Mr. Martin ducked his head. "I know what it looks like, but I wasn't coming here."

"It's none of my business."

An awkward silence fell. He licked his lips. "I just don't seem to be able to give you the right answer about anything." Suddenly, he pulled his hat off and pressed it to his chest. "Look, I've gotten off to a bad start with a lot of people before, but this has to be the worst. And I'd like to apologize."

He sounded honestly contrite. A little crease just above his left eyebrow, almost covered by a sprig of molasses-colored hair, argued for it. Abigail decided she could be magnanimous. After all, things were looking up for her, ironically in part thanks to this mail-order fiasco.

"Apology accepted. I think everything is turning out for the best."

At least for me.

What a shame Mr. Martin was a shiftless, no-good drunk. She wanted to shake her head in pity, but refrained. All the wasted potential. To her surprise, Abigail realized she was a little disappointed.

~

Looking down into her clear, sparkling, green eyes, Oliver saw her disappointment in him. Worse—he saw pity. Things were turning out all right for her, sorry she couldn't do anything to help him—a hapless drunk. That sympathetic, bless-your-heart expression said it all, and it made him sick.

He'd wanted to take Wilkins apart for touching her. Not out of crazy jealousy or anything. The lack of respect was unacceptable. She deserved more. She deserved chivalry. And for the first time in a long time, he'd wanted to fight for something.

Mrs. Holt made Oliver…want to be more than he was. A man worthy of her respect, but why bother? She wouldn't look past her list of qualifications to see any good in him.

"Mr. Martin, I don't mean to be forward, but…" Her stomach growled and her cheeks reddened. She was even prettier when she blushed. "I know you paid for my meal the other night. I've been eating sparsely because of my lack of funds—"

She was going to ask about the two hundred dollars. The woman was a bulldog, he'd give her that. But John could pay it. He'd gotten them all into this mess. "John'll be by to talk to you about that. Good day, Mrs. Holt."

He didn't exactly run, but he abruptly excused himself from her presence, her little pink mouth forming a startled *o*.

~

Oliver settled in the corner of Sonny's Saloon with his beer and heaved a great sigh. Funny, he wasn't even thirsty — especially at this hour—but he just wanted a minute to think before he went back to that stupid, cold creek. Of course, he didn't really have the time. Time was money, and he and John needed to hustle to get little Miss High Standards squared away.

Oliver was only a little surprised at himself for clocking Wilkins. The man had it coming. He'd needled Oliver over and over, but only when Oliver was drunk beyond responding capably. So there was a pattern to Wilkins's behavior—he picked on the weak. Women and drunks. Today it had ended. And Oliver felt better about himself.

A little.

Mrs. Holt, unfortunately, had seen nothing noble in his temper.

"Little early for a drink, ain't it?" A soft, sultry voice asked.

Oliver looked up into a pair of pretty, but haggard, brown eyes. Marlene. One of Sonny's upstairs girls. Oliver had been to see her. Once. Right after Avonia's stunt. And she'd made a habit of asking for repeat business.

"Morning, Marlene." Oliver pulled his beer closer, then pushed it away. He didn't wish to be rude, but he also wished the woman would drop it.

Twirling her index finger in a long, caramel curl, Marlene pulled her robe tighter and sat down with him. "I was gonna have Bill fry me up an egg with a slice of sourdough. You hungry?"

"Nah, not really. But thanks."

She seemed embarrassed by her state of undress and kept tugging the robe tighter over her bosom. "Oliver, you know, you've only come to see me once. In my profession, that can give a girl an idea. Like, maybe you weren't all that happy with me."

He dragged a hand over his mouth, buying a moment to think. He'd been so drunk… Maybe she was used to hearing that. At least it seemed like a kind excuse. "I had an awful lot to drink that night…I barely remember anything…"

"So, it wasn't me?" She sounded almost hopeful. "Nothing I did wrong?"

Oliver honestly didn't know how to answer her. Was she fishing for some kind of compliment on her professional skills?

"I mean…" She cleared her throat and shifted in the chair. "You haven't been with any of the other girls, either.

It's not…I mean, it's just not something you make a habit of, is it? That's it, isn't it?"

Still perplexed at what she was getting at, he shook his head. "No, ma'am." Then, Oliver wondered if partially explaining himself might get the woman to leave him alone. "I was dealing with a pretty big blow that day. I had a moment of weakness."

"You regret it." It wasn't a question.

Oliver thought of his ma, John, and, strangely, Mrs. Holt. "No reflection on you, Marlene, but I was raised better. I hope that doesn't hurt your feelings."

Marlene smiled at him, but it was tinged with sadness. "Not at all. In fact, I'm glad to know there are still a few good men around here."

An involuntary snort escaped Oliver. He knew a lot of people who would disagree with her assessment.

Marlene laid a hand lightly on his arm. "I know what people say about you. But they're wrong." She winked at him and rose slowly to her feet. "Good men like you always come back to their senses. I would know."

CHAPTER 4

Abigail closed the print shop every day promptly at noon for her lunch break. Only today, she would use part of that time to send a telegram. Once a week, she checked on her boys.

Locking the door and tucking the key into her reticule, she meandered along the boardwalk, nodding or saying *hello* to the few townspeople with whom she now had a passing familiarity. A block down from the print shop, she crossed the intersection and strode toward the Western Union office.

The door opened as she reached for it and a tall, handsome, young man with piercing dark eyes nearly walked into her. "Oh, my apologies, madame," he said, snatching his bowler off and stepping back to hold the door for her, his dark, brown hair askew now. "How clumsy of me."

His gaze lingered and Abigail blushed at his open expression of appreciation. "Not at all," she said, slipping past him. She approached the counter harboring the sense that the young man was considering something, talking to her, perhaps. She truly hoped he wouldn't. A moment later, she heard the door close and smiled with relief at the clerk.

"Wednesday already, is it?" the elderly gentleman with amazingly thick spectacles asked.

"It certainly is." She pulled the pencil and pad on the counter closer. "I would wire my boys every day if I could afford it. Every day." A lump unexpectedly tightened in her throat and she dropped her blurring gaze to the paper.

Apparently noting her distress, the little man patted her hand. "You take your time writing that up. I'll just be over at my desk."

Mercifully, he stepped away and Abigail took a moment to reclaim her emotional balance.

Surely, not much longer, Lord. Soon, I'll have them with me. Soon. Thank You so much for the job that will enable me to send for them.

Seems it never failed. If there was a person Oliver didn't want to see, sure enough, that was the person he ran into every trip to town. And he ran into Mrs. Holt as she was coming out of the telegraph office.

They stared awkwardly for a moment, then Oliver remembered his manners. "Mrs. Holt." He tipped his hat. "Good afternoon."

"Good afternoon."

The tension between them stretched on and she raised her chin, as if daring him to fix it. His gaze shot past her to the telegraph office. "Checking on your boys?"

"I just sent a telegram to their school, yes."

"Ah."

They danced around each other for a moment on the boardwalk, but of course they were heading in the same direction. No way out of it, they began to walk together.

"Your boys," he said, desperate to fill the uncomfortable silence and stop the conversation from going back around to the money. "How old are they?

"Nine and eleven."

"Eleven. Well, he's almost a man."

"Yes, he believes so, anyway. James is a take-charge kind of boy. Athletic. Lanky. A bit too fiery, I fear, but honest and moral."

"And the other?"

"Artemus is thoughtful, deliberate, somewhat athletic, but out of necessity rather than natural ability. And straight as an arrow."

"Do they miss their father?"

Mrs. Holt drew in a deep breath. Sadness etched its way into the crease between her eyebrows. "The last few years were difficult. Sebastian's drinking increased. His temper increased. His patience with the boys decreased." She shook her head. "Those were difficult days."

"I'm sorry. I didn't mean to pry."

"No," she squared her shoulders and raised her chin again. "Water under the bridge now. We're moving forward. If I marry again, love will have nothing to do with it. I will marry a good man or I won't marry at all."

Oliver didn't think she meant to dig at him, but he felt the barb, nonetheless. He was not a good man by her standards. Maybe by no one's. Except Marlene's.

They approached Telegraph Street and Oliver touched the brim of his hat to excuse himself. "Always a pleasure, Mrs. Holt. Good day."

He'd meant to ask about her plans. He'd meant to ask what she thought of Jubilee Springs. However, he'd lost the desire for conversation, with her or anyone else at the moment. Besides, she was bound to bring up the money again.

She raised her hand as if to stop him, but he pretended not to see and stepped off into the street.

Of course, in another twenty feet, he ran almost straight into Landers. Both men stepped back, startled, then Landers looked Oliver over, kind of slow, like he was taking an inventory. "I'd heard you quit drinking. That true?"

"Pretty much, yeah." The only reason Oliver answered the impertinent question was that he felt he owed the man something for disrupting a perfectly good poker game—a game Landers had been winning.

"Also heard about Wilkins." Landers was looking at Oliver with a tight, suspicious gaze. "You gonna turn out to be more trouble sober than drunk?"

"Not unless you give me any reason, I guess."

Landers seemed to ponder the answer for a moment, running his tongue over his teeth. Finally, he nodded. "Reckon that's fair enough."

"Reckon so." With that, both men continued on their way. A strange exchange, but Oliver had the idea maybe Landers would be more careful around him than Wilkins had been.

~

Ice water swirled around Oliver's bare feet as he dipped his pan. At least today he didn't notice the cold as much.

Regarding Mrs. Holt, he ruminated on the woman a bit too much, he supposed, but he didn't have two hundred dollars.

Looked to him like she had even less, and he did worry about her. For two days, he'd pondered on how to get her the money. She had a right to it. He agreed with that, but he didn't have it.

He hated to ask John for it. He should, seeing as how all this was his fault. But he just didn't want to.

Getting angry again, he sloshed too much water over the sides of the pan. At least he caught sight of the glittering flake and plucked it out.

He was loath to tell Mrs. Holt he didn't have the money. Especially since he knew he *should* have it. He was already lower than an alcoholic minister in her estimation of men. She didn't need to know how he'd been frittering away his time here in Jubilee Springs. And to have John clean up this mess, though it was of his making, made Oliver want to spit nails.

From the knees down, he was numb. His fingertips ached from the icy water. He hated making a living this way—if you could call a few flakes here and there a living.

Oliver glanced up the stream at John, squatting near the shore, wet from the waist down, examining something in his pan. He was always cheerful, always hopeful. And he had said for years now that there was gold in Oliver's future.

He gave a snort of disgust, deposited the flake in the leather pouch on his hip, and scooped a little more gravel. "Gold, Lord," he whispered. "John's always been so sure I'll be the one to find it." He dumped out some water, swirled the pan again, gently sloshing the gravel around and around. "If I am gonna find it, can I pray that it's sooner rather than later?" Not really joking, he straightened up, arched a sore, stiff back. "How much longer you gonna work?" he hollered down to John, sifting in a pool forty or so feet away.

"Think I'll work till dark."

"What about supper?" John did all the cooking, and Oliver was getting hungry.

"You take that nice gal Mrs. Holt to dinner. Tell her what we decided. Smooth things out with her and don't run from the conversation again."

Oliver nearly threw his pan at John. "You've bumped your head. If anyone should be buying her dinner, it's you." Besides, he'd already bought the woman some meals.

John straightened up and leveled a hard gaze on Oliver. "She's here alone, on her own, away from her family, and it's our fault."

"Our fau—?"

"Now you take her for a good, full meal and smooth things over with her. Tell her we'll pay the money if she's still of a mind not to marry you. Only we'll need to make it in four payments, like we discussed."

Well, she certainly didn't want to marry Oliver. And he sure as heck didn't want to pay her the money. "And the two hundred dollars is coming out of your stake, not mine."

"If you feel it should, fine."

John's quick acquiescence made Oliver suspicious. Then the scrapes, the saloon tabs, the apologies, the feathers John had smoothed, especially in these last several months, rushed at him like a flash flood. The true debt, who owed whom, wouldn't be forgotten. "How about fifty-fifty?"

John bent down and dug a scoop of gravel. "Shave before you go. And wear something it don't look like you slept in."

~

"You're punctual. I appreciate that."

Oliver stood in the doorway of Mrs. Holt's room, his hand still hanging in the air after knocking on her door. She had opened it almost instantly, as if she'd been waiting anxiously. She was expecting him?

"You look confused, Mr. Martin. Mr. Fowler's note said you'd be here at six."

Oliver's jaw clenched like a bear trap. *Dang that meddling John Fowler. How'd he known? Pulling my strings like I'm a puppet.* "Six. And I'm here. At six. I take it you're ready?" He motioned to the shawl draped over her arm and a reticule hanging from her wrist. "I thought we would eat downstairs."

"That's fine. I enjoy it. Thank you for the meals you've sent."

He didn't respond. In silence, they ambled along the hallway and down the stairs to the inn's restaurant. Oliver had the urge to comment on how nice she looked in a simply cut, green dress covered in little pink flowers. The bustle was much smaller than he'd seen her wear before, but the color brought out her eyes to the point they were nearly mesmerizing. She had her hair, all the glistening, golden waves of it, pulled back at the base of her neck with a matching green ribbon.

But he wouldn't say a word. No sirree. She'd made it plain she was too good for him. He glanced down at his striped shirt, its wrinkles betraying its normal resting place —a tight space in the back of his drawer. He had at least shaved.

And none of this mattered one iota. They'd hammer out some final details over dinner and part friends...or something of the like.

As they waited for their meals, the silence stretched on unbearably. She bounced her fork. He tapped his fingers. She licked her lips. He sipped his water. Suddenly, they both spoke at once.

"I apologize for being insensitive—" "I'm sorry if I sound greed—"

They stopped, but a little chuckle escaped them and Oliver thought it broke some of the tension. "I'm sorry." He snapped his napkin open and spread it in his lap. "Ladies first."

"I was only going to say I'm sorry if you think I'm greedy and money-grubbing."

"No, I never thought that." *Liar.*

"But you must think I sound anxious for you to pay me the money for breaking the contract."

"For the record, I didn't break it. I never would have applied for a bride in the first place."

Her face tightened a hair, but she persevered. "I understand your position. Do you understand mine? Even a little."

"Yeah, I do," he admitted grudgingly. "That's what I started to say. And I'm sorry John brought all this on us."

She seemed to ponder that a moment. "Originally, I was furious, especially after meeting you."

"Back to those qualifications again."

"You weren't what I was expecting, and then to find out it was all a lie...frankly, it could have been devastating to me."

"I'm glad you got over your disappointment so quickly."

She ignored his sarcasm. "I think coming to Jubilee Springs may turn out to be a Godsend. I have acquired employment." She bit her lip, as if considering a decision, then folded her hands over her placemat. "Mr. Martin, I got desperate back in Atlanta. The bills were piling up. My children seemed lost. Our home felt as if it were coming undone.

"This mail-order bride idea took hold in my brain and wouldn't let go. I was especially taken with the notion that I could, so to speak, *design* a husband and father."

Mr. Martin pulled back from the table. "And avoid your previous mistakes?"

"Yes. You see, I didn't think I had any other options. I hated the idea of a menial job that would barely allow us to eek by. If I was going to do that, why not simply get married? I decided to draw a picture of the kind of man I wanted to live with, someone who would be an excellent father, and see if God delivered."

"Sorry to disappoint."

"You did, but God didn't."

Oliver found those little stingers she kept delivering, no matter how unintentional, more and more annoying.

"Now that I have decent employment," she continued, "I can take a little more time to think about things. I can provide for the boys and me. With the money you owe me, I can rent or buy a home and bring them out in a month or so. Much sooner than I had dared hope."

"Got it all planned out, don't you?" He admired her for her spunk and deliberation. She didn't take hardship lying down. But she was still young and pretty. The right man was going to come along and she'd sweep those plans under the rug in a hurry, he'd bet. "What if you meet a man who can stand up to your list?"

"My children do need a father, Mr. Martin. If I marry again, it will be for them."

On one hand, it sounded like a waste of a young and vibrant life. On the other, Oliver could understand Abigail's aversion to love. Hadn't been anything but trouble for either of them. "You seem awfully optimistic about this new job. Where are you working?"

"At Mr. Stewart's print shop. My father owned one when I was younger. As a result, I am an adept typesetter."

Stewart? Oliver had heard something about the man, something not so good. His doubt must have danced across his face.

"Is there something I should know about Mr. Stewart?"

She pleaded with her eyes for him not to say anything. There was some vague rumor or gossip Oliver had heard about the printer, but for the life of him couldn't recall it. That's what he got for staying drunk too much of the time. He decided he could be wrong. "No. I was, uh, just trying to remember him, is all. Tall fella? Skinny? Older?"

"Yes, that sounds like him."

The waitress arrived with two steaming plates filled with steak and potatoes and Mrs. Holt dove in. Oliver hid a grin behind his coffee. She was trying to be delicate and use her manners, pinky in the air and all, but she sawed into that steak like it might try to run. Her attention fixed on the food, and for the next several minutes, nothing else seemed to exist. Oliver cut a bite of his own steak and was more than pleased with the juicy, salty flavor.

"I had lunch with Mr. Fowler the other day," she said between bites. "He thinks so highly of you."

"He's been a good friend for a long time."

"How did he know your father?"

"They both ran small ranches in New Mexico. My pa was killed in the earliest days of the Lincoln County War. Nobody even knows whose bullet. Afraid for us, John sold his ranch and brought Ma and me to Colorado. We kind of partnered up on two small spreads just outside Durango. My foreman is running them both right now."

"Why did you leave your ranch?"

Avonia. Another name for Satan. He didn't say that, however. "I needed a change of scenery. John came to Jubilee Springs to visit me and wound up staying. He'd like to go back, though."

"Why doesn't he? Oh—because he's worried about you."

"I haven't been the sharpest tool in the shed in the last year. I've done some pretty stupid things. John's…had my back, you could say."

"He believes in you. Very much."

"Yeah, that's one thing about John." Oliver stabbed his steak and cut. "His hope springs eternal."

"At least you have someone. A friend." He looked up at the comment, but Mrs. Holt just as quickly dropped her gaze. That awkward silence crept back in.

He cleared his throat. "Mrs. Holt, why don't you go back to Atlanta? We'll give you your money. Go back to your people, your children."

"My brothers and sisters are scattered across the country. My parents are gone. I believe Jubilee Springs is where

God wants me. It's a fresh start for me. Us. The town is becoming our home." She straightened in her chair. "As a step toward that new start, I would like to formally release you from the marriage contract."

Though she didn't mean it in such a way, Oliver supposed, he felt *rejected*. A foolish emotion. Just his pride talking.

Regardless, it was a good first step, a way of speaking her resolve. Well, he had some things to resolve, too. "I'll leave some money for you at the inn's front desk in the morning. We'll make four payments if that's agreeable."

"What is the time frame?"

John hadn't mentioned that. "How about two months?" The time had fallen out of the sky and he grabbed it. Why not? Two months, two years. Either way, it was a tall order.

"That's acceptable." She offered her hand to seal the bargain.

They shook, and Oliver was amazed at how tiny and delicate her hand was...and how warm in his. Natural feeling, even. Like he'd held it before.

He broke their grip abruptly, rudely, and rose. "Goodnight, Mrs. Holt."

Abigail brushed her hair in front of the window.

Backed by the darkness of night, the glass afforded at least a weak reflection of her from the lantern light. Over and over, she pulled the brush through shimmering locks of gold, while she pondered Mr. Martin.

Dinner had been an unpleasant affair. They just

couldn't seem to find comfortable footing with each other and he had departed so abruptly. Again.

What is it he's running from, Lord? Help him stand and face it.

The irony that she had found her future here in Jubilee Springs due to a happy accident that had consequently tied Mr. Martin in knots wasn't lost on her. Not to mention, she believed the situation was straining his friendship with Mr. Fowler.

At one time in his life, Oliver was all those things you're lookin' for in a man.

Her hand slowed, dragging out the brush strokes.

Once upon a time.

I thought maybe you'd help him find himself again...I believe you're the perfect woman for Oliver.

The idea was absurd.

Yes, she noticed the few weathered lines in the corners of Mr. Martin's sapphire eyes. And the way his unkempt chestnut hair swept in multiple directions around his head at once, even though he'd combed it. Nor had it escaped her attention that Mr. Martin had shaved for dinner, revealing soft, clear skin not grayed with razor stubble. More intriguing, he'd made an attempt to iron his clothes. A somewhat futile effort, as most of the wrinkles remained.

A little half-smile lifted the corner of her lips.

Yes, he could use a wife.

She blinked. *But not me, Lord. Oh, no, not me.*

I'm a typesetter now, not a mail-order bride.

CHAPTER 5

Oliver squatted and reached his hands out to the open door on their pot-bellied stove. Winter might come early to Jubilee Springs this year since summer hadn't had a chance to spend more than a few hours here so far. He dreaded another day, summer or otherwise, of wet, cold feet, blue fingers, and a stiff back. But they'd committed to a year. He'd give it his best shot.

John barged in, his arms full of wood. He kicked the door closed with his foot and Oliver backed out of his way so he could drop the load and throw a few sticks on the fire. "So," his friend asked, shoving wood into the flames. "You smooth things out last night?"

Oliver shoved his hands into his pockets and shrugged. "I guess enough. She's got a job. And I told her we'd pay her two hundred dollars inside two months."

"A job, you say? Where?"

"Stewart's print shop."

"I heard somethin' about him."

"That's what I thought." Oliver moved around so he

could see John's face. "What? What did you hear? I can't remember, but it was something."

Rubbing his chin, John narrowed his eyes. "Yeah, it was something...to do with Landers, wasn't it?"

Oliver snapped his fingers. "That's it. He owes Landers money. Lost a lot to him in a poker game."

"More like Landers cheated Stewart out of it."

"Nah. I played against him one night. Stewart's reckless and can't bluff worth a darn."

"Hmmm." John moseyed over to the kitchen table, spun a chair around, and settled in front of Oliver's cup of coffee. "Why two months?"

"What?" For a moment, the zig-zagging conversation lost Oliver. "Oh, I don't know. Just...came to me."

"How 'bout we each go ahead and give her fifty dollars. That should help her with a house to rent, or a room, or to get her kids out here."

"Agreed."

John downed the coffee and stood. "Let's rustle up some breakfast. Then we'll go out and see if today's the day we find a big nugget."

Oliver held back a disgusted snort. Barely.

Abigail honestly wasn't sure what drew her to an abrupt halt—the woman with her hands resting on the shoulders of two young boys, clearly her sons...

Or the way the family was laughing and chatting with Mr. Martin in front of the leather shop.

Hugging the freshly printed box of stationery to her chest, Abigail stared longingly at the group. The mother was a very attractive young lady with glistening, chestnut hair piled atop her head. Her two boys, so close in age to James and Artemis, were as redheaded and freckled as Irish fairies. How the picture of the little family tweaked her heart. She missed her boys so much.

Yet, simultaneously, she felt a twinge of disquiet. The family seemed to have an unmistakable and affable familiarity with Mr. Martin. Their laughter, the way the woman smacked him on the shoulder, the way Mr. Martin ruffled the shorter boy's hair.

A woman carrying a parasol bumped into Abigail, snatching her attention back to the boardwalk and the stationery in her arms.

"Oh, I'm so sorry," she said, walking passed Abigail.

Abigail merely smiled politely but let her gaze drift back ahead to the gathering. At that moment, Mr. Martin saw her and smiled. "Mrs. Holt, I'd like you to meet someone."

Waving her into their group, he stepped back a little. Abigail felt she had no choice and walked the few yards up the boardwalk to them. "Yes, hello." She nodded at the woman and the boys.

"These are my neighbors," Mr. Martin said. "Lucy Madden and her boys, Josiah and Johnathan."

The three of them exchanged pleasantries, but Abigail couldn't get rid of an odd and unexpected awkwardness. "Well, it's lovel—"

"Lucy is looking to take in mending," Mr. Martin interrupted. Something in his eyes said there was more to be told, but he wouldn't say it.

"Yes, I'm very good with a needle," Mrs. Madden added.

"Well, thank you for letting me know. I'll be sure to find you should I need anything tailored."

Mrs. Madden nodded warmly. "Thank you. Well, we must be going. Thank you again, Oliver. Nice to meet you, Mrs. Holt."

"Yes. You, too."

For some reason, when Mr. Martin didn't move, neither did Abigail, and they both stood quietly for a moment, watching the family walk away. She couldn't help but wonder about his relationship with the woman. It wasn't her place to ask, of course. Or was it?

"Is she the reason you balked so firmly at my arrival? Are you two—"

"What?" Mr. Martin seemed to choke on the question. He removed his hat and raked a hand through his hair—coffee-colored hair in need of washing. Abigail scolded herself for the assumption.

"She's a widow, like you," he volunteered, pressing his hat back in place.

Abigail wasn't sure how she should feel about that. Foolishly, her pride reared up. He was concerned about Mrs. Madden, but he wouldn't marry Abigail? She flinched at the ridiculous thought. "Was her husband also a drunkard, like mine?"

She didn't miss the hint of shame in his expression as he hung his head.

"I take it he was one of your drinking buddies?"

Mr. Martin slipped his hands into his pockets and looked at Abigail. "We tossed a few back, yeah. I got him in trouble a few times, cost him some money."

Sebastian had spent more time with those kinds of friends than with his family. They never seemed to be in short supply. Perhaps her disdain for the memories showed on her face.

"She could use the money," he mumbled. "I think being a widow—it's going to be harder for her, though, than for you."

Abigail was intrigued. "Why so?"

"She's not as…" Mr. Martin seemed to flail for words, but finally settled on, "flinty as you."

Abigail pursed her lips but didn't respond. Nor did she disagree with the word. She'd sensed a softness in Mrs. Madden. Life had worn her down, not sharpened her to a keen edge. The pressure of widowhood might crush her. Abigail, on the other hand, had grown stronger, but had she become too razor-like as well, slicing those around her with careless comments?

"Maybe that was out of line. I'm sorry." Looking a touch contrite, he backed up a step. "Well, I guess I'll go look for some gold." Abigail did not hear any enthusiasm in his voice, only weariness. Touching his hat, he turned and walked away.

But his observation echoed in her head and left her feeling ashamed.

She's not as flinty as you.

A couple of hours later, his feet numb and fingers blue, Oliver straightened up and stretched. The August sun felt good on his shoulders, but dang, he was tired of spending his days bent over a pan full of water and gravel. He should be doing more with his life. He had a good ranch. What was he doing here with ice water in his boots?

Those annoying little qualifications of Mrs. Holt's buzzed around in his brain. She sure was picky. Unreasonably so. Only…Oliver had to admit, something had changed in him this last year. A year ago, he wouldn't have seen her list as any real obstacle. He wouldn't have cared what she thought about his drinking buddies or anything else he did.

A year ago. Before Avonia?

He used to bypass alcohol, but now found solace in it. He cursed more than he ever had. And he'd even had a dalliance with a soiled dove.

Financially, his ranch had made him more money than this panning. Yet here he was, hoping for a strike rather than tending to a good herd. And what little he had managed to save—well, looked like it was going to go for the hotel room for Mrs. Holt and the penalty for breaking the contract. She was right to point out his temper, too. Somewhere along these last several months, his fuse had gotten pretty short.

He was going backward.

"By the way, Lucy is taking in mending and wash," John said, as if aware Oliver needed a distraction. "I'm gonna take her a couple of shirts."

"Yeah. She told me."

A few minutes later, John tried again. "So what is Mrs. Holt doing for Stewart? Clerking?"

"Typesetting." Oliver wasn't distracted. He was agitated. Like he wanted to run. Wanted to see new scenery. Exactly the way he had felt when Avonia jilted him.

"Hope those rumors about Stewart are wrong," John was saying as he lifted his pan out of the water. "That would be bad if she was caught in the middle of something."

Oliver hadn't really heard him. All he could think of was this growing feeling he had to outrun something, get out of town and clear his head.

Now.

"Listen, John." He waded out of the water. "I heard a rumor of a strike a few days over in Rifle. Thought I'd go check it out. See if there's any truth to it. If we could get there before the hordes flooded in—"

"We might get there before it's panned out?"

"That's what I was thinkin'."

"Worth a look, I reckon. How long?"

"Just a couple of days."

"Think I'll ride along. Unless you were wantin' to spend time alone."

"No." *Just wanted a change of scenery.* "I could tolerate your ugly face. You might scare off the bears."

John didn't react to the barb. Instead, he dumped his pan. "I'll go ask Lucy and her boys to keep an eye on things here for us."

"I'll go exchange some of the dust for coins and get the horses. We'll head out tomorrow."

"Early."

"Early," Oliver agreed.

Abigail looked up at the sound of the bell and smiled. She had mixed emotions about Mr. Fowler, but had settled in her mind that his intentions had been good, if not wise, and meddlesome, but not villainous.

"Good morning, Mr. Fowler." She dropped the word *August* in place on the composing stick, then laid the type aside to meet him at the counter. "What brings you by?" She bit off an inquiry about the money.

Pulling his hat off, he surveyed the print shop, decidedly neater now that Abigail had tidied up a bit. "Stewart in?"

"No, I'm sorry. He's delivering some menus. He shouldn't be long."

Mr. Fowler waved away the man's absence. "No matter. I come to see you anyway." He approached the counter and reached into his breast pocket. "Oliver and I are fixin' to go out of town for a few days." He laid a small stack of cash on the counter. "This is our first payment toward that two hundred dollars. I wanted to get that to you…"

He trailed off and Abigail thought she heard something somber in his voice. She stared at the money, surprised by a vague pang of guilt, but tried to shake it off. They'd had a contract. Mr. Fowler and Mr. Martin had violated its terms. Besides, this was for her boys. She picked up the bills. "If it wasn't for my sons…" she tried to explain.

He shook his head, salt-and-pepper hair gyrating. "No, ma'am, I want you to have that. Funny, it seemed important to bring it to you before we left. Guess I wanted to make sure you'd eat while we're gone."

He chuckled, but Abigail wasn't sure she heard much humor in it. "Is everything all right, Mr. Fowler?"

"Right as rain." He winked. "See you in a few days." He dropped the old, tattered hat back in place and nodded goodbye.

Right as rain. Somehow, Abigail didn't think so.

She stared out the door a moment longer, watching Mr.

Fowler cross the street and turn left. His visit—or was it his departure—left her with a strange melancholy.

Lord, I pray Your protection over Mr. Fowler. And Mr. Martin.

The prayer made her feel better, and she knew work would also help lift this gloomy mood. She had one small order of wedding invitations to print today, some ads to lay out for the upcoming inaugural edition of the newspaper, and a legal notice for Mr. Shields, an attorney.

Mr. Stewart could take his time coming back.

Retying her apron, Abigail strode into the back room to get a fresh jar of India ink. She passed Mr. Stewart's desk and noticed an envelope there with her name on it.

A little finger of fear poked her stomach. No reason the envelope should disturb her. Perhaps Mr. Stewart had left her a bonus. She snatched it up. Inside, she found only a brief note.

Mrs. Holt, I sincerely apologize for the inconvenience about to befall you. You have been an impeccable employee. Unfortunately, I owe a great deal of money to someone in town and am unable to pay the debt, even with the increase in business you have precipitated. In fear for my life, I am leaving. I have left money in the register. Please take your pay.

CHAPTER 6

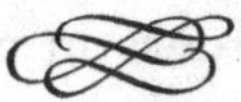

Abigail collapsed in Mr. Stewart's chair and stared at the note. He had just…left? What was to become of the shop? Her position here?

This debt. How large was it? Could she get a loan and pay it herself?

Pay yourself first.

The thought was clear and urgent. And it was logical. She had worked now for several days. Mr. Stewart had even been planning on paying her today. She knew what he owed her. And she had his blessing.

She rose and rushed to the cash register at the front counter. She supposed her urgency was due to the stress of the situation, but she felt she had to hurry. Quickly, she counted out the fifteen dollars, closed the drawer, and tucked the money away in her reticule beneath the counter.

All right. It's all fine. That and the money Mr. Fowler left will hold me for a bit while I look for another job.

Disappointment dogged her. *Lord, I was so enjoying this position.*

Why—

She didn't follow through on the thought. *Whys* didn't matter, and she trusted God.

She supposed with no employer, she had no job, but customers had placed orders in good faith. The least she could do was finish them. After that—well, she'd take it one day at a time.

Two more customers came in that day. Abigail didn't turn them away, but she didn't promise delivery either. She said she'd check the work schedule and see what *they* could do. Please check back.

Abigail spent her time in the shop printing and praying, and waiting. *But, Lord, what am I waiting on?*

Using her brayer, she inked the type for the wedding invitation lying on the plank and then cranked the type into position beneath the heavy platen.

Can I keep running the shop? But how? It's not mine. Is there any way?

She pulled the Devil's Tail down, the heavy platen impressing the image on the paper, then raised it back. The bell rang, signaling another customer. "I'll be right with you."

She laid the invitation in the stack with the others and strode to the desk. "Yes, sir. May I help you—?"

An older man, dressed in black, removed his hat and raised a sinister face. He had piercing dark eyes and a lift to his lip that looked too much like a sneer. "Stewart. I need to see Stewart."

"He's not here at the moment. Could I give him a

message?" The man approached the counter and laid a hand on it. A short, fat stogie smoked between his fingers. "How long's he been gone?"

Abigail wasn't sure what to say. Perhaps the truth. "He left this morning to deliver some menus."

"That usually take all day?"

"I don't know what restaurant they were for." She shrugged, knowing the explanation was frail.

"Hmmmm. Well, if he comes back here, you tell him Landers wants to see him. 'Course, I have a suspicion I'll have to find him. In the meantime..." Landers swung round behind the counter, shoving Abigail out of the way. He dropped his hat back in place, snatched open the cash drawer, and grabbed all the money.

"See here," Abigail protested. "This is robbery."

"No, it ain't. He owes me a lot more than this. But I'll be back. I'll collect it." He slapped the counter, dropping ashes on it, and strode to the door. Just as he opened it, though, he stopped and turned. "You can tell the sheriff if you want. Don't make no difference. I got Stewart's IOU in my pocket. This wasn't stealing."

He winked at Abigail then slipped out.

She waited just a moment to make sure he was gone, then swept the ashes into the waste basket. Rubbing at the tension in her brow, she dropped onto the stool. She wanted to stay. She didn't want to leave. She didn't want to look for another job. She wanted to run this print shop.

Could she?

What if that man kept wandering in and taking money?

An audacious idea formed in her brain.

Lord, it's not illegal. I wouldn't take any pay I'm not due, and

I would save the rest for Mr. Stewart, if I can, if he comes back. I'll just...stay the course. I'll tell people he had an emergency and will be back as soon as he can. And I'll keep a lot less money in the cash register.

~

Oliver let himself into the assayer's office and had to wait a moment for the clerk to finish off with a customer. Nothing to do but stand there, Oliver noted the fella's tailored suit and new, clean bowler held to his chest. He was young, mid- or late-twenties maybe, dark hair, dark eyes. Probably just the kind of man Abigail would like.

"Yes, the quality of the ore is quite stunning," the young man said in apparent agreement with the clerk, Walter Cramer. "Mr. Birmingham and Mr. Hallmark will be gratified to hear that. I've already begun the legal paperwork to register a new poinçon pin for our metals specifically."

Oliver could tell he was educated, too. Sounded like it anyway.

"How long will that be?" Cramer asked, scratching his head beneath his visor. "'Cause if you want a special stamp on your bouillon, I'll have to keep your ore separate from everybody else's."

"Will that be a problem?"

"Space." Cramer dropped one hand on the counter and motioned to the room. "Depending on what you send me, I'm liable to run out of space." He glanced around his small building, all of about five hundred square feet. It was filled with shelves of ore in burlap bags tied with identifying tags.

The back wall supported a counter on which sat a pair of scales, a distiller, dozens of beakers, flasks, and Bunsen burners, along with a hundred or so small bottles of chemicals and two large cans of Nitric Acid, all for testing the ore.

The man surveyed the one-room office with a frown. "Hmmm, I see." His gaze landed on Oliver and he dipped his head in apology. "I'm so sorry. Why don't you conduct your business while I…" His stare drifted back to the one-room building, cramped with shelves of ore. He didn't finish his thought but he stepped out of the way.

Oliver laid a bag of dust on the counter. "Cramer, I wanna get some coins for this." He nodded a hello to the guard standing quietly in the corner, his rifle draped across his chest. "Hannigan."

The man nodded back.

Cramer, a short, round man who had always reminded Oliver of an affable pig, tossed the bag up in the air and caught it. "All righty. Give me just a minute." He turned around and stepped over to the scale he kept behind the front counter.

Oliver leaned on the wood and eyed the fancy fella studying the office. "None of my business," he began slowly, "but Cramer here doesn't use but about a third of this counter." The stranger turned to Oliver, listening. "You could cut out the waste, make room for a safe."

The young man inclined his head, as if the idea intrigued him. "A safe, yes."

"I've heard what's coming out of Birmingham and Hallmark's mine. I wouldn't want it mixed with this dross in here, either."

The man walked up to Oliver and extended his hand. "I'm William Blakely, the new attorney for Birmingham and Hallmark Holdings of New York."

"Oliver Martin." The two men shook.

"I appreciate your suggestion. I think it's a fine idea. And since Birmingham and Hallmark Holdings own this building, I wouldn't think there would be any problem with the change."

"Probably not."

"Here ya go, Oliver."

Cramer presented him with two stacks of coins and the leather pouch. "A hundred and five dollars and six cents. That all right?"

Oliver counted it out quickly and dropped the money in the bag. "Have to do."

"Mr. Cramer," Blakely pointed at him. "I'll be back in a few hours. With a carpenter."

The little man nodded, his expression bland, as if he didn't care one way or the other. Oliver and Blakely left the building together. On the porch, which did not have a roof, Oliver tugged his hat a little lower against the bright morning sunshine. Beside him, Blakely tapped his hat into place.

"Mr. Martin, your suggestion was quite helpful. Could I buy you some lunch to show my appreciation?"

"It was just a simple idea."

"Yes, but compared to what I was thinking, it was also far more productive."

Oliver raised an eyebrow, waiting for an explanation.

"I was thinking we might need to build an entirely new building."

Oliver chuckled. "Eventually, maybe, but not in the

short-term." The two men started walking, ambling down the porch steps at an easy pace. "And about lunch, I was heading to the café just to get some sandwiches for a trip. But I thank you for the offer."

"Well, would you mind if I accompanied you there? I'm still new in town and haven't discovered any place but the restaurant at my hotel."

"Sure." Oliver knew what it was like to be some place strange, unfamiliar. Fortunately, all his life, he'd had John to buddy around with. How much colder and lonelier must a place be when a man had no friends around at all? "Come along. The roast beef on sourdough alone is worth the walk."

Oliver shifted in the saddle, trying to give his weary rear end a rest. He'd been off a horse on a regular basis for too long. Aside from the soreness, though, he was thoroughly enjoying being out on the trail. The scent of pines in the air, mountain views that went on for miles, and comfortable summer temperatures that made outside work a pleasure—yep, he missed his ranch.

He'd needed this little trip. A chance to think about who he was once and what he had turned into. He felt his head clearing already.

"Have I changed that much, John?"

"Changed?" John nudged his horse and the animal trotted up beside Oliver. "No. You've just lost your way. I believe you'll come back around to it."

Ever hopeful. Ever optimistic. Oliver had to smile. "Just get back in the saddle."

"Yep."

Thunder rumbled across the valley and Oliver looked back at the setting sun peeking at them from between a massive thunderhead and the mountain ridge. Not long before one or the other blotted out the light. "We should find a place to camp. Looks like we might get wet."

"I came through here a few years ago when I brought that herd up from Montrose. I don't think we're too far from an old miner's hut. It ain't the Palmer House, but it oughtta be dry."

A half-mile up, they left the main trail and followed what amounted to little more than a deer path. It led down the steep sides of Grizzly Mountain to a wide, grassy flat beside Snowbow Creek. The rain almost beat them. Oliver and John had time to throw their bedrolls and saddle bags inside the cabin before the bottom fell out of the sky. A torrential deluge hit. They hobbled their horses back up in the pines, then ran for the cabin. Shedding wet coats, they settled in for a meal of cold jerky and hardtack.

The cabin leaked like a sieve, but the men managed to find roughly a twelve-by-twelve area in the corner that only had a few leaks instead of gushers. Glad to be dry, Oliver leaned back against the wall and stared into the deepening shadows.

The cabin was a wreck. The floor buckled and tilted in multiple directions. As far as furniture, one splintered chair sat in pieces next to the crumbling fireplace. Half the wall beside the river rock chimney had rotted away and was gone. Or maybe a tree had fallen on the fireplace, causing all this damage. Oliver wasn't sure. Regardless, water poured down the remnants of the rock chimney, blew in from the opening, and pooled in the middle of the floor. The thunder bounced off the steep mountainsides with deafening crashes. Oliver had never heard such a storm.

A sense of foreboding slithered up his spine.

Shaking off the gloom, he tore a bite of jerky and tried not to wish for a steak. "Well, I'm glad we found this place, even if there's no stove." He had to raise his voice to be heard over the rain.

"Agreed. It's a mean storm. Peculiar for this time of year."

After a quiet meal, John scrounged around and found a lantern tucked beneath the broken chair. "Hey," he said, shaking it gently. Oliver heard the kerosene. John smiled and fished a match out of his pocket. The stormy gloom disappeared in the warm glow of the lamp. "Not much kerosene in there, but enough for us to see a couple hands of cards."

"Good idea."

John set the lantern down beside them and Oliver pulled a deck of cards and a small bag of buttons from his saddle bag. With quick, sure movements, he divvied up the buttons and dealt the hands for draw poker.

Oliver gathered up his cards. "I never did ask you. How did you settle on Mrs. Holt?"

"I read her letter. She was pretty clear on what she wanted in a man. And I know the man you *were*. Struck me you were both lookin' for the same thing...you could do a lot worse, you know."

"I did. And that was enough for me."

"You can't judge every woman by that cotton-headed Avonia. You were struck dumb by a pretty face. You ain't the first. But you've learned your lesson. You can see through the pretty little smiles and enticing curves. Now judge a woman the same way you'd judge a man. On her character."

Over the years, John had given some good advice. This was maybe the best.

"If God smiles on ya"—John laid down two cards and Oliver slid him two more—"He'll send you a woman with integrity *and* nice to look at, at the same time."

Oliver admitted grudgingly to himself that Mrs. Holt had character. And she *was* mighty pretty to look at.

"If you weren't so bent on running from love, you'd see what a treasure she is."

Oliver shrugged. "Maybe I don't want to see. Maybe I just don't think it's worth the punch to the gut." For a moment, he thought about letting his friend win the hand. Instead, Oliver laid a royal flush on the box.

John groaned and tossed in his cards.

"Maybe my luck is changing." Oliver swept the buttons to his side.

"Your love life could change, too, if you give that girl a chance."

Oliver shuffled the cards and dealt another hand. "You haven't been listening. Besides, she has standards. I don't measure up."

"Ah, that's only 'cause she don't know you. If I could give you one piece of advice, Oliver, that I know you'd listen to, it would be to court her. Do something to show her the man you are. I guarantee she'll like what she sees."

"Sometimes, John, I think you're getting Old Timers. Won't be long before I have to tie you to the front porch so I don't lose ya."

John laughed at the notion and anteed up. "I hope I live

that long. I hope I live long enough to see you married and bouncing babies on each knee. Wish your ma would have made it."

Oliver sighed. "Yeah, me, too."

"Life is short, son, and it goes by quick. You can't live it nursing a grudge."

Was that all his affection for Avonia had netted him? A grudge? A bruised ego? He'd sulked long enough, he supposed. Sulking was the right word, too. Unable to throttle Avonia, he'd tried to choke the life out of himself. In retrospect, he'd been pretty stupid. "Just didn't know what to do with the anger…and the embarrassment."

"Her fickle heart saved you from a life of misery. Next time you see her, you should thank her." The lamp flickered, dimmed. "Looks like we're going to bed." The light gasped one last breath, then died, plunging the cabin into inky blackness.

"Dang," Oliver whispered, groping for his bedroll. "It's dark. I can't see—" As if obliging his search, lightning lit the cabin for an instant. "There it is."

He took advantage of the flash and settled down for the night. "See ya in the morning, if we don't float away before then."

John grunted. "Heck of a storm for this time of year. Usually don't see rain like this till September." His rustling sounds slowed, then stilled. "Night, Oliver."

Cold and wet. The uncomfortable sensation tugged at Oliver. It made no sense. How could he be wet in his bed?

The instant the thought formed, the cabin screamed,

water roared, lightning flashed. Oliver saw the building collapsing on them, pushed by an angry, exploding wall of water. Then darkness again. A solid, suffocating absence of light and air stole the breath from his lungs, muffled the cacophony of destruction.

He tried to scream—*John!*—but the sound was strangled and full of bubbles. Water rushed into his mouth. He tumbled, over and over, thrown about like a twig by the force of the water. Something rammed into his ribs and pain rocketed through him. He broke the surface into darkness, splashing, clawing, grabbing.

"John!"

The relentless river pulled him down again, slammed him into an immovable object, maybe a boulder, forcing the air from his lungs. Jealous, the angry current snatched him past it. He swam wildly, reaching out, grasping for anything solid and unmoving, but the water roared on, thundering around him like a bellowing titan.

It carried him away, fast, in complete darkness. The crashing water deafened him. Something else hit him in the leg, hard, and he felt the charley horse. Then, to the back of the head, another vicious blow, and Oliver Martin gave in to the river.

Cold. Cold like he imagined death would be. Pure. Deep. Biting.

A violent shiver hit Oliver, bringing him to some semblance of awareness. His arms were around something. His shoulders ached and burned. His face—no, his right eye—throbbed violently. His fingers stung, as if he was holding onto to something icy hot.

He couldn't make sense of the sensations.

Wake up, stupid. Open your eyes.

He swallowed and blinked, focused on…

Tree bark?

What the—

He pulled back a little and realized he was hugging a tree. Confused, he looked around, and his heart dropped to his stomach. Water, swirling and hungry, raced by not five feet below him. Debris piled up around the trunk, as other bits and pieces floated past.

He sat perched on a slender branch, his arms and one leg around a young poplar. The other foot, bare and blue from the cold, rested on a smaller branch. His toes were swollen. The nails were broken, jagged, and smeared with dried blood.

Below his foot, water. Churning, dirty, debris-clogged water. And he knew what had happened.

Flash flood.

"John," he whispered, surveying the flooded landscape. He was only twenty or so feet from shore. Other trees nearby stood battered by the water, their lower branches draped in waste…but empty of life. "John," he tried calling, but only managed a raspy croak.

He shook his head. *Think, Oliver. Think. Flash flood. You made it to a tree. The water is already dropping. Shore isn't far. Just hang on a little longer.*

"Oh, God, where's John? Please let him be all right." He prayed with desperation. "Please let him be all right."

He forced down the knot in his throat, fought the rising

panic back, and ignored the numbness in his extremities. Moving slowly, stiffly, he lowered himself from the tree. The water was just as cold as before, but he didn't care. He was headed to shore. He would find John. He had to be all right.

The current was still strong but not insurmountable. He half-stumbled, half-swam his way over rocky ground to the shore and climbed to dry land. The sun was peeking over Grizzly Mountain, but between passing clouds. It had a long way to go to offer any warmth. Shivering violently but noticing it only in the back of his mind, Oliver slogged up the shore. He ached everywhere, intensely, like a herd of buffalo had trampled him. His hands were white and marred with ugly, throbbing cuts. His toes, bruised and swelling, bled afresh from shattered toenails.

None of it mattered.

John. Where are you?

He hobbled upstream, hoping, praying John was there, perhaps looking for Oliver?

He scanned the little grassy flat where the cabin had been.

Only slightly higher than the stream, the plot was no longer underwater. But nothing remained to encourage Oliver. The rushing water had scoured away the existence of the camp. Not even foundation stones remained. No sign of the cabin's existence had survived. Had it even been there?

Was this some terrible dream?

Oliver ran a stiff, aching hand through his hair and turned to scan the river. John could have been swept miles downstream—

An arm, white as the belly of a dead fish, poked out of

some foamy rapids on the other side of the stream. Tangled in debris and a blue Indian blanket.

"No, no, no!" Oliver thrashed and splashed his way across the stream, astonished at the rate at which the current was subsiding. "No, no, no," he repeated, but within a few feet of the arm, he could see that the hand was missing its ring finger.

CHAPTER 7

Guilt, anger, grief, and even fear stalked Oliver's mind as he fought to remain calm and untangle his friend from the tree root. He wouldn't look at John's face. Just touching the ice-cold, bluish-white flesh nearly stole his reason. He couldn't look into his friend's dead eyes.

"Just get him out of the water." In the flood, John had lost his shirt and his boots. "You shouldn't be buried like this, John. I'm sorry." He would give him his shirt. He wouldn't bury his friend half-naked. No dignity in that.

Oliver was vaguely aware of these nonsensical thoughts as he pulled his friend's lifeless form free of the eddy, tugged the body to the shore, and dragged him up onto the sand. "You were a good friend, John. I'm sorry. I'm sorry." A sob unexpectedly tore loose from Oliver. Weeping, he hugged his friend and gave in to the grief.

Tears blurred his vision, choked his voice as he settled on his knees. "I'm sorry." He couldn't say it enough. He hugged John tighter and rocked back and forth. "You were supposed to take care of me. You've always taken care of me. I'm so sorry."

Oliver remembered the sound of a rifle, a bullet ricocheting off an adobe wall, and a hand slipping from his grasp. Only five years old, he'd stood dumbfounded in the middle of the street in Lincoln, New Mexico, as his father fell to the ground and his blood seeped into the dirt. John had come from nowhere, swooped Oliver up like an eagle, and deposited him behind the garden wall of an adobe house.

He'd rescued Oliver and his mother from what would become the bloody Lincoln County War and had kept up his thankless guard duty for years. Until it had ended here in a remote, forgettable stream high in the mountains. It all seemed such a waste. To die for someone like Oliver—a rambling, lost, ne'er-do-well. Worse—a *boy* nursing a bruised ego.

Oliver sat holding John till time lost its meaning. His tears spent, his heart broken, his mind numb, he acknowledged the time had come to dig a grave, and he gently laid his friend down.

He knelt a few feet away and commenced shoveling. He scooped armful after armful of sand and gravel off to the side. He would dig deep. He would give his friend of many years a quiet, safe resting place.

With every sweep of his arms, he saw John alive, vibrant, breathing. He could hear his laughter, see him riding a pony across the fields at the ranch, recall him splashing ice-cold water on Oliver as they panned in the creek.

Flinching under the weight of the memories, Oliver dug and dug until he encountered a large rock. A piece of quartz. He scooped out the sand around it to determine a handhold, a way to lift it out. He traced the edges. Dug some more.

Where did it end? How big was it?

Regardless, it would have to come out. Something rose up in Oliver—a furious, irrational refusal to start the grave over. He would move this rock. He would give John Fowler a safe, deep grave if it was the last thing he ever did.

A horse neighed, and his head swung up. Oliver's mount stared back at him from a cluster of cedars. She looked wet and shaken, but was alive, and the saddle still hung on her. Which meant Oliver's mining pack did, too.

Calmly, whispering in hushed tones, he extended his hand and limped over to his horse. "Sophie, that's a good girl. Shhhh." Sophie grumbled and stepped back. "Whoa, girl, whoa. It's all right." Moving toward her with slow, deliberate movements, Oliver grabbed her halter and led her down to the water. "Get yourself a drink, girl." The irony of the offer worked a disgusted snort from him. "Yeah, I guess we've all had enough water."

Clenching his jaws to keep his emotions reined in, he pulled his shovel and pick from the mining satchel. He rolled a sore shoulder and went back to work.

He swung the pick, loosening the ground. He sweated. He shoveled. He tugged. He pushed. He worked the rock back and forth. Over and over.

The storm clouds had dissipated, and the sun, directly above now, beat down on Oliver. He paused to wipe his brow and rest for a moment on his shovel.

Without his shadow covering it, Oliver noticed more details of the rock. In the stark sunshine, parts of it—*gleamed*? He jumped in the shallow hole and wiped sand

and clay off a section. Beneath the soil, the rock was yellow. One might even say…gold.

~

Bathed in sweat, Oliver finally heaved and rolled the rock up onto the edge of the grave. Mouth open in awe, he pulled back from it. Working the mammoth piece of quartz free had taken him nearly all day. Finally, there it sat—a piece of white quartz easily the size of a buffalo's head… one *riddled* with streaks and *chunks* of gold.

What did it weigh? Seventy pounds? Eighty? Even if only a fourth of that was gold, he was a rich man. His gaze drifted over to John, now wrapped in his bedroll. "You were right. Ma was right. I found the gold." He had never suspected those words would be so bitter and painful. "I won't let you down. Or Ma." He raised his eyes to heaven. "Or You. I know Your hand led me to this spot. You're giving me a second chance to be the man I've been running from. I'll take it."

~

Oliver finished wrapping the monstrous nugget in a blanket and heaved it up into his arms. Still amazed at its heft, he struggled over to the makeshift travois and set it on the canvas. Sophie grumbled, as if well aware pulling this back to town was not going to be any fun.

"Yeah, sorry, girl," Oliver said, patting her on the rump. "But I'll feed ya oats covered in molasses every day for the rest of your life if you get this gold to Jubilee Springs." He stepped up and pulled the reins from her back. "And I'll have custom boots made." He looked down at his foot wrapped in a shirt and frowned. "A pair for every day of the week. Come on." He tugged the reins and Sophie obeyed. The goals seemed so frivolous and he spoke them with no conviction.

Together, he and his faithful horse took their first trudging steps forward. He almost looked back at John's grave but didn't. No more looking back.

The slog was slow going. It would take two days to Jubilee Springs. With every step, he had a memory of John to recount. From the violence-filled streets of Lincoln to Oliver's spread next door to John's in Colorado. Both ranches had been kind of small, but they'd teamed up, sharing land, water, and hands. Within a few years, both ranches were running at a healthy profit.

Ma's unexpected passing, followed closely by Avonia's jilting, had thrown Oliver for a loop. He'd been so convinced that a change of pace, of scenery, of goals would fix everything, and he'd rushed here to the gold fields.

He shook his head in disgust, grunting. The noise startled a flock of finches from a mulberry bush and Sophie started. "Whoa, girl." He patted her jaw and spoke softly. "It's all right. I said I wasn't looking back. What's done is done. John would tell me to buck up and look up."

Oliver squared his shoulders, got Sophie moving again, and tried to lighten his steps. Look up? To what? Unfortunately, Mrs. Holt's face drifted to the surface of his muddled thoughts. Admittedly, she was never that far away from them. His desire to see her, the way she was linked with thoughts of John, made no sense. But he wanted to call her a friend. She had liked John. Perhaps that was why—

The thought was cut off by a twig snapping somewhere up the hill. Surprised but attempting to hide the reaction, he pulled Sophie to a stop and listened. A bear or a cougar would have the horse prancing. Watching her ears move as she tracked the sounds in the forest, Oliver eased back a foot and slid his rifle from the scabbard. The animal was calm, but obviously listening to something.

Oliver sensed company up in the pines. He could feel the eyes on him. A moment later, a man tugging a mule behind him stepped out of the trees about fifty yards away. The beast was loaded with pans, shovels, a tent, and saddle bags full to bursting. The man carried a rifle in his left hand, but kept the barrel pointed at the ground.

"Safe to approach?" The stranger called. "I seen ya pull out your rifle. Don't mean no harm. Just looking for a little company."

Oliver did not want company. He did not want to talk. He definitely did not want to explain what was riding on the travois. Mayhap the man wasn't on his way back to town. "Which way you headed?"

The man started ambling down the hill. "Jubilee Springs."

Oliver wilted. He couldn't say no. Unless the stranger exhibited bad behavior, but thus far, he had been polite and careful. "Come ahead." He would not put down his rifle, of course, just in case.

The man was an older fella, near as Oliver could tell. His face was covered with a wild-and-woolly gray beard. His matted, salt-and-pepper hair hadn't seen a barber in months, maybe a year, and it shot out crazily from beneath his tattered felt hat. His clothes were threadbare and hung on a spindly frame.

Oliver knew the type. The miners that haunted the mountains, panning the creeks alone, convinced they could find their own strike. It did happen, occasionally. Most of the time, though, these men just wound up spending too much time with nobody. It made them…odd.

The stranger drew up beside Oliver and Sophie and offered his hand. "Jeremiah Dumas."

"Oliver Martin." The two shook and started their walk again. "You look like you've been up here a while."

Jeremiah scanned Oliver and his less-than-perfect condition, pausing on his bootless foot. "You look like you've had some trouble."

Oliver nodded. "Flash flood. Had to bury a good friend a ways back."

Jeremiah clucked. "Yep, that's the way of these mountains. Take, take, take. Give back very little."

Oliver did not respond, merely nodded. Jeremiah half-turned and studied Oliver's rigging, his gaze staying for a moment too long on the rock. Oliver never went looking for trouble, but this man was curious. As was his timing.

"Looks like you're taking something home, though."

Oliver decided to lay his cards on the table. He stopped and turned to the man, raising his rifle between them. "Mister, my friend died, but you could say he left me something. Beyond that, I don't care to discuss it."

The old man's eyes, pretty much hidden by the brim of his hat, glittered, and he raised a hand in apology. "Don't mean to intrude. Just making conversation."

"Make it about something else."

The two men held each other's gazes for a moment, but then Jeremiah ducked his head. "I can happily talk your ear off about something else."

~

Oliver had managed to tolerate Jeremiah's incessant chatter till about six in the evening. They'd found a campsite on a high bank above the river, and Oliver excused himself to tend to his throbbing toes in the icy water. Jeremiah had volunteered to fry up some apples and a little bacon. Not much of a meal, but they were only about ten or twelve miles from town. Tomorrow, they would be back in civilization and have some real food.

Glad of it, Oliver sank his swollen, black-and-blue-toes into the frigid creek and flinched at the bite, but then sighed as the cold numbed the pain. Yes. Tomorrow. A big day. He would find out what that gold was worth. Find out what his friend had died for.

And, no denying it, he was eager to see Mrs. Holt.

Before he could delve into the unbidden thought, he thought he heard Sophie grumble. The ripple and rush of the water made things hard to hear, but he knew his horse. Grudgingly, Oliver rose from the water, limped up the hill—

And wanted to smack himself for being so stupid. So trusting.

Jeremiah had unwrapped the rock and was attempting to lift it. To what? Run off with it? Nobody, man nor mule, was getting anywhere fast lugging that monster. But more importantly, Oliver had a debt tied to that rock. No one was going to take it.

Period.

He'd left his rifle in the saddle, his .44 draped around the saddle horn. The only chance he had was to sneak up on Jeremiah. He had to cover thirty or so feet quietly, quickly. He picked up a rock, lobbed it past the horses, and moved. The noise drew Jeremiah's attention long enough.

Oliver clambered like a frantic, injured spider across the clearing and grabbed Jeremiah's arm, snatching it. Startled, the old man spun as the cumbersome rock slipped from his arms and landed on his foot. He howled, and Oliver flinched but took advantage of the opportunity and shoved Jeremiah to the ground.

"What do you think you were doing, old man? Did you really think you'd get far with an eighty-pound rock?"

The old miner clutched his foot, howling in pain. "Dang, I think it's broke."

"Serves you right."

"You can't blame me. Look at it..." Jeremiah's gaze shifted to the white quartz rock marbled heavily with streaks of gold. His expression changed, softened, took on more of a dreamy look, but something dark and hungry glittered in his eyes. The face of avarice. "I don't suppose you'd want a partner? Or maybe you'd at least tell me where you found it?"

Oliver almost choked at the bold and audacious requests, but bit it back. Instead, he saw an opportunity to get rid of his company. He had not staked a claim at John's grave, solely because he did not want to tip off anyone who might pass by before he could return. Therefore, the odds of finding the right spot were pretty dang high.

"That whole section of creek was littered with rocks like that one."

Jeremiah's eyes bugged and he jumped to his feet, his injury all but forgotten. "Whole section? Section where? Which creek? Bear Creek or Ruby Rose Creek?"

"Ruby Rose. A couple hundred yards before the falls." Not a lie, but a broad generalization, to be sure.

Excitement shone in the man's eyes, but then his brow dove. "Why would you tell me that, boy? You puttin' me on?"

"I staked my claim. I'm not entitled to any more without a partner." It was a gamble, but not much of one. If Jeremiah went back and found his own nuggets on such vague directions, he deserved what he dug up. In the meantime, Oliver knew the nugget he already had was filled with more gold than most men panned in a lifetime. He may not ever return to the spot for the purpose of finding more of the metal. Though he would return…

Jeremiah licked his lips and turned away, limping over to the empty travois. "I'm sorry about my greed. Don't know what came over me."

"Greed," Oliver said flatly. He couldn't imagine how a nugget like this might have wrecked him if he'd found it under normal circumstances, even with John still alive. Now, Gold Fever was the last thing he'd catch.

"Well, uh, if you don't mind"—Jeremiah scratched his head beneath his hat, looking deep in thought—"yeah, I believe I'll turn back and head on up that way."

The man was practically salivating. Oliver was relieved to lose the company, but disturbed by the change he saw come over the miner. "Be dark in a few hours. You won't make it back in time."

"No, no, that's true." Jeremiah moved a little quicker over to his mule, the injured foot seemingly getting better by the second. "But I'll be halfway 'fore I have to stop."

Oliver watched the man trek with obvious, gnawing

obsession back down the trail, the way they'd come. And something told him, *but for the grace of God, there go I...*

CHAPTER 8

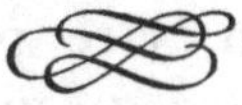

Abigail did not sit idly by, expecting business to come to the print shop. There was the newspaper, and it held potential for substantial income. However, with Mr. Stewart gone, she would have to write a few articles for it. Therefore, she needed to organize her thoughts, her days, and her goals. Wasting daylight was akin to sin, her father used to say.

Eager, therefore, to get an early start on her day, she slid the key into the print shop's door before dawn and let herself in. She would not do anything outside the purview of her current employment. She would take only her salary and spend money only on bills and expenses associated with the shop. She would write it all down, keep meticulous books. If and when Mr. Stewart returned, Abigail would be able to account for all his money.

But now, her lunch hour would have to be about more than selling ads. She needed something to write *about*. With a few ideas bouncing around in her head, she worked the press that morning, finishing off one order, then closed for lunch and headed to the café.

She discovered quickly that the citizens of Jubilee Springs all had some story to tell, some event to promote, some meeting to announce. The Irish American Club president was eager to announce their Wednesday night dinners. Mrs. Sorenson, vice president of the Ladies Quilting Association from the Presbyterian church, was looking for donations of scraps for baby quilts. The Millers wanted to share the news of their daughter's engagement.

Before Abigail could leave with her sandwich, she also had the notes for an announcement from the Merrimons. They were delighted to announce that their new building had been rented by a photographer. He would be opening for business in time for Christmas portraits. Mayor Lewis shook her hand, offered her a polished, professional smile, and promised to drop off an article regarding his thoughts on incorporating Jubilee Springs. Dale Boggess, seeing the interest in the newspaper, asked about an ad for his café.

On and on it went over the next few days as the news spread of the newspaper and Abigail's need to fill it with interesting articles. Content for the paper, it turned out, would not be a problem. Best of all, she would have to write very little of it herself.

Late one afternoon, she sat down at her desk—Mr. Stewart's desk, she reminded herself, and looked at her notes for the first issue. She'd typeset about half the paper and had enough articles and announcements here to finish it. Not much longer, and she would have the *Jubilee Bugle* on the press.

Abigail was pleased with the name, but the smile on her face felt a little sad. All this had come about because Mr.

Fowler had attempted to help his friend get his life back on track. Instead, he'd wound up helping Abigail. She would hug the man when next she saw him.

She drummed her fingers, musing over Mr. Martin and Mr. Fowler and their steady friendship. At least they seemed to know how blessed they were to have each other, and Abigail envied them. She missed her boys, couldn't wait to have them with her, but simple, enduring friendship—well, it was something she hadn't had in a long while.

She prayed that Mr. Fowler and Mr. Martin would be good friends their whole lives.

Oliver and Sophie slogged their way into Jubilee Springs mid-afternoon the next day, the horse dragging the travois loaded with his gear and the quartz wrapped in a worn, unassuming, old blanket. He rode right up to the assayer's office and trudged inside, his bootless foot still wrapped in a shirt. His footsteps were as heavy as his heart, but it was time to take care of business, make better, wiser decisions. Think with his head and not his heart. At least for the moment.

"Cramer, I've got somethin' I need help with." The clerk looked up from the gold he was weighing and eyed Oliver with a pinched expression. Hannigan stood in the corner with his rifle, watching them intently. "I've got a rock I want kept in your safe. I'll come back tomorrow and work the gold out."

"Whatcha got? Some quartz with a little gold in it?"

Oliver motioned with his head. They stepped outside,

and he flipped the blanket back. "More like some gold with a little quartz in it."

Cramer gasped. His eyes bugged, and he dropped to his knees beside the rock. "Holy jumpin' Jehoshaphat, where'd you find that?" He ran his hands over it as if it were the Holy Grail. "No wonder you want to put it in the safe." He paused his hands. "What do you reckon you got?"

Oliver quickly flipped the blanket back over it and pulled Cramer to his feet before too many people on the street noticed them. "I won't know till I bust it loose from the quartz, but I'm guessing maybe fifty pounds."

Cramer whistled again. "Holy smoke, if that's right, you ain't ever gonna have to work another day in your life."

Ironically, Oliver had plans to do just the opposite.

Oliver was in rough shape. He stared at himself in the mirror, none too pleased. His dark hair was stringy with dirt and oil. He had nearly a week's growth on his face. His blue eyes were dull with fatigue and sported gray smudges beneath them. A few fading, black-and-blue bruises dotted his cheekbones, souvenirs from his tussle with the flooded river. He looked terrible.

And all he wanted was to see Mrs. Holt. Hadn't been able to think of anything else but her and John, like they were linked somehow.

Oliver had seen a kindness in her face, heard it in her voice, when she talked of John. She would care about his death. And he wanted to tell her because he needed someone to share his grief with. It puzzled him that he should feel this way, but he'd had some time to think about things. He was lonely. Without his friend, he was lonelier still.

Behind him, reflected in the mirror, one of John's shirts hung on a peg. That red-and-black plaid he liked so much. Oliver would never wear it. Then what would he do with it? With any of John's things? A simple enough question, yet he had no answer. Maybe she would know.

He bathed, shaved, poured some iodine on his toes, and dressed in the cleanest things he had—a dark blue, double-breasted button-up and a canvas pair of Wahmakers. He'd worn this the day he'd proposed to Avonia and had not put it on since. He had no delusions about romantic entanglements with Mrs. Holt. In fact, the choice of clothes had less to do with her and more about the change in him.

Dressed, he grabbed his tan Stetson from the hook and strode from the cabin.

~

"Mrs. Holt."

Leaning over a tray of typesetting letters, fingers hovering, ready to pluck a word free, she looked up at the sound of his voice. Oliver was enormously pleased to see her smile reflect genuine warmth.

"Mr. Martin." She straightened and met him at the counter, hand outstretched. "You're back."

"Yes, ma'am." Remembering his manners, he snatched off his hat and shook her soft, warm hand. "Unfortunately, I have some bad news."

Her face paled. "My boys?"

"What? No."

"Of course not. I'm sorry. You wouldn't know anything about them. A mother's reaction."

"Yes, ma'am. No, I came here to tell you about John."

"Mr. Fowler? Has something happened? Is he all right?"

"No, ma'am." Oliver had thought this would be easier. His throat tried to tighten up on him. Almost angry with the unexpected reaction, it took him a moment to fight it back.

Apparently, Mrs. Holt saw his struggle and came around the counter. She touched his arm and gazed up at him with compassion. Immediately, a sense of well-being flooded Oliver, like he got when he hadn't been home to his ranch in a while and saw it off in the distance. Like coming home…

Her eyes, green as a spring pasture, evoked a strange mix of desire and tranquility in him. A tiny wrinkle in her forehead expressed compassion and concern, and Oliver clung to what it might mean like a lifeline.

Unconsciously, he leaned a little closer to her and imagined his hand caressing her cheek.

"What's happened to Mr. Fowler?" she asked gently.

Oliver recalled the jarring image of John's arm poking out of the water and flinched. "He drowned." She gasped and squeezed his arm. For an instant, he was lost in the pain in her gaze. She had cared about him. "I buried him up in the mountains."

"What happened? Can you talk about it?"

As long as she didn't let go. It amazed him how a woman's touch could bring him so much comfort. Maybe he was so much lonelier than he knew. Or maybe she touched his soul. "We were spending the night in a miner's shack near Snowbow Creek. Rain hit about sunset. I've never seen it come down like that. I don't even remember what happened.

"I came to in a tree, and John was dead." That lump tried to come back to his throat. To hide his pain, he turned and marched over to the window. "Anyway, I think you liked him…a little. I thought you would want to know. I hope I haven't imposed by telling you."

"No, of course not, and I'm glad you did. I'm so sorry for your loss." She came to stand beside him. The scent of lilacs followed her. "I know he meant a lot to you, and I truly did like him. Under different circumstances, we would have been great friends, I believe."

Oliver didn't respond, just stared out at the street and the passing traffic. He wanted to get a marker for John's grave. He'd do that before he went back to the assayer's.

"He stopped in here the morning you left. Did you know that?"

That surprised him. "No. He didn't mention it."

"He came by and left me some money. His countenance troubled me. He seemed…I don't know, a bit melancholy. And he even mentioned it seemed important to bring me the money before he left." She smiled sadly. "He said, 'Guess I wanted to make sure you'd eat while we're gone.'" Her chin quivered.

"That sounds like John." Oliver scrubbed his face, trying to make sense of it all. "Well, you don't have to worry about that anymore. I'll pay you all I owe here in the next few days."

"Please don't trouble with that now. It's not important. You need to deal with this first."

Yes, he had quite a lot to deal with. "I don't know what to do."

Somehow, she understood what he meant. "Does he have family? They'll want to know. And his personal belongings. You'll need to go through them. Determine what to keep, what to send to them. You may even donate some things, like his clothes."

He nodded, pleased she could think so straight, and she had given him a plan. "I'll write some letters this evening. He had a wife in Omaha. I think she'd want to know. I'll donate everything else, minus a few items."

"Please let me know if there is anything else I can do to help."

"Would you? I mean, willingly? Or're you just being polite?" He held her gaze, wanting an honest answer.

"No, I truly liked Mr. Fowler. And I have an odd…" She shook her head, as if searching for the right word. "An odd sympathy for you. It's not your fault we're *entangled,* so to speak. I shouldn't hold this mess against you. I think we can be friends."

"I could use a friend about now."

Her eyes widened slightly, perhaps she was surprised by his honesty. "Me, too."

He started to go but stopped. It felt right to tell her the whole story. "Do you believe in God, Mrs. Holt?"

"Absolutely. Very deeply."

"The strangest thing happened when I was diggin' John's grave. I found a gold nugget. I don't mean something the size of a marble, either—"

"Something that was hard to miss?"

"You could say that. What do you think about such a find?"

"As a Believer, I think it was a gift. I think He was just

letting you know He was there with you in your grief. That's how I would look at it, anyway."

Oliver nodded, unsure what God was thinking or trying to tell him, but he did know God's hand was in all this. Mrs. Holt clutched his arm again. "I'm not the only friend you've got, Mr. Martin. There's One who holds you closer than a brother. Remember that."

He didn't respond for a moment, marveling over the emotions her touch stirred up in him. The way her voice—easy and sweet like warm honey—poured over his heart. Yes, there was no other word for it. She made him feel peaceful, like the thought of coming back to God.

And he hadn't been at peace in a long, long time.

CHAPTER 9

Abigail tried to focus on her work. She had at least two orders she could complete today. Concentration, however, was in short supply. One minute she was sifting through the lead type, building a word or sentence, and the next her mind had drifted. To him.

Like now.

She blinked and plucked the word *and* from the box of type and set it on the chase, the frame that held the item she would print. Oliver—*Mr. Martin*—had looked different. She didn't attribute the change to his grief, though that was heartbreaking enough. No, something had changed in him. She hoped for the better. He struck her as serious, or perhaps *focused* was more accurate.

He was alone now, too, and she felt for him. His grief tugged at her heartstrings. She had wanted to hug him so badly, to whisper words of comfort to him. She could imagine it too easily. Oliver would be warm and safe in her arms. She would feel the muscles flexing in his shoulders, the softness of his hair against her cheek—

She shook her head and backed away from the images in her mind. Surprised by the direction of her thoughts, she wrapped them up neatly in denial and excuses. She was hurting for him and longed to show him some compassion. That was all.

His grief reminded her of the *proper* response. He had specifically said he needed a friend. She had no choice but to try to be one.

She was fearful that calling on him might muddy the waters between them, but not visiting him in this dark time would be the height of insensitivity. Just a quick visit, to let him know she...cared.

Of course she did. As a friend.

So she found herself at sunset staring at a small, one-room cabin on the edge of the Arkansas River. A picnic basket of food from the restaurant hung at her elbow. She had asked for directions from a clerk at the inn. He had said she would know the cabin by the picture of Lincoln on the front porch. An oddity, but there it was, a photo of the president from some twenty years ago.

To whom did it belong? Mr. Fowler or Oliver?

She flinched at the slip. Why was she having trouble thinking of him by his formal name? Mr. Martin. No matter. She swept away the trivial concern and marched up to his door.

The boards squeaked beneath her boots as she raised her hand to knock. She heard something slide on the floor —probably a chair—and Mr. Martin opened the door. His raised eyebrows and round eyes almost made Abigail laugh.

"I take it I've surprised you."

"Yes, ma'am, you could say that. Um, what are you doin' here?"

She almost joked that not making a bereavement call was an unpardonable sin to a Southerner, but decided humor would be insensitive. "I brought you a meal. I'm sure you don't feel much like cooking, in your grief."

"Oh." His gaze fell on the basket. "You cooked?"

"No, I'm sorry, I did not. At present, I don't have a way to." She lifted the basket. "This is from the restaurant in the hotel."

"Oh, well, thank you." He stepped back. "Please come in."

"I can't stay long, of course," she said, crossing the threshold. The cabin was small and lacked much light, but it was neat. Tidied and swept, at least. The beds were made. She set the basket on the only table in the room. Envelopes, several sheets of paper, and a pencil waited in front of one of the chairs. "Letters?"

"Yes. That was good advice you gave me." He left the front door open and joined her at the table. "One to his wife, one to his sister, and one to our foreman. You think of anybody else?"

She shrugged. "If he had a will, you might want to contact his lawyer. If his hometown has a newspaper, you could write an obituary." Abigail knew that when the words left her mouth, she would be sure to include one in the forthcoming issue of the newspaper. "And I'll publish it. I'll have my first paper out in a few weeks."

"That soon? You certainly have been busy since you hit Jubilee Springs. That reminds me..." He quick-stepped over to the counter and untied a leather wallet. He fished around inside for a moment and pulled out a small stack of cash. "Here. This squares us, I hope."

"No, I really don't want to think about money at a time like—"

He clutched her hand, pressing the money into her palm. Her breath caught in her throat. His gentle, calm, but grief-stricken expression pinned her still. "There's something you should understand. The nugget I found when I was digging John's grave…it probably weighs over fifty pounds."

Abigail couldn't keep her eyes from bugging. "Fifty *pounds*? Are you sure?"

"And I think that is a conservative guess." His hand tightened slightly on hers, and he moved a hair closer. He didn't seem to be aware of it, but she couldn't help but notice his nearness or the heat of his hand.

He searched her face, and she wondered what he hoped to find. "I won't miss this. In fact, I should give you more. John and I caused you a lot of heartache. I'll help you bring your boys out. If you're staying, it's the least I can do."

Abigail heard him speaking, but for a moment couldn't hear his words. Her attention had wandered to his sad eyes, blue as a mountain lake, his smooth, clean-shaven jaw, and slightly damp, *combed* hair curling toward his face. Her hand in his, warm, gentle, safe.

His touch seemed to complete a connection between them.

She gasped and stepped back, but he held onto her hand. His brow dipped in apology. "I'm sorry. I didn't mean to offend. I thought that would be a help."

She pulled her hand away, but he made sure she took the cash. She turned her back to him and pressed the money to her breast. She wanted to scream at herself for being stupid, vapid, drawn in by a handsome face. *Remember, at one time, Sebastian had been handsome, kind, and gentle.* "No, no, I'm sorry. Your offer took me by surprise, is all."

"Mrs. Holt—" He cut his words off, as if thinking them over.

When he didn't restart, she rounded slowly. "You were saying?"

"I—I, uh, I was wondering if you would help me write the letters."

For some reason, this didn't ring true. Abigail wondered if he had started to say something else. "I'm not familiar with the family."

"I never met his wife or his daughter. They didn't communicate. And I wasn't going to be long-winded. Just let them know he had passed, and I would forward anything he might have left them."

"Did Mr. Fowler have anything of value?"

"His ranch, but we were partners. And we had a death clause. I suspect he might have had a little money set aside. They'd be welcome to it."

"Well, I don't think you want to say that in the letter, at least not until you know for sure." She slipped by him and sat down in front of the pile of paper and envelopes. "I'm sure the attorney will contact them if there is anything to inherit. You could say that."

"Yeah." He sat down across from her.

Sunset's light streamed in from the window beside them, bathing him in a warm, almost mystical glow. As if Heaven had opened up and was pointing a divine light on him. They stared at one another. Abigail sensed he wanted to say something, something important, but was holding back.

A dark curl fell across his forehead. She wondered what it would feel like to run her hands through his hair, caress his cheek—

She swallowed, alarmed at the direction of her thoughts. "Why don't you write the letter to your foreman? I could write the one to the ladies, if you like." He nodded but didn't move, merely kept his gaze trained on her. Abigail felt so strange. He made her almost breathless. "A nugget that big. You've been given an incredible opportunity. What will you do with it? Have you thought that far ahead?"

"I know that I want to make John proud. And I know that God gave me this chance for a reason. I don't plan on letting them down. I'd—I'd like..." He licked his lips and started over. "John gave me a piece of advice. I might take it."

"What was it?"

He didn't answer, but she felt like an explanation was hanging in the air. After a moment, he rose and walked to her side of the table. Gazing down at her, he reached out and touched her cheek. Abigail's heart hammered in her chest. Her breath came in shorter and shorter gasps.

Slowly, gently, he took her hands and pulled her to her feet. They stood so close she could feel his breath on her face. Her gaze dipped repeatedly to his mouth. How could she so easily imagine a kiss...?

Oliver dropped his arms to his sides, and a cold wind blew over her. She wanted him back. She wanted the heat he promised, but that was playing with fire. She knew better.

Didn't she?

"I know you don't think much of me, but I'm a better man than you give me credit for."

The words hit her like a slap in the face.

"I'm a better man than you think, Abigail." How many times had Sebastian drunkenly bellowed out that sentiment? And then tossed back another beer or whiskey? "I'm sure you are. I'm sure—" She stopped, fighting the bitterness that had instantly crept into her voice. A man had to die for Mr. Martin to recognize his foolish ways.

Abigail wanted to kick herself for coming too close to this flame. Sebastian had promised to be a better man over and over. Stop his drinking. Get his anger under control.

"Next, you'll tell me you'll quit your bad habits. You won't stop at the saloon after work. You'll be home every night in time for dinner." Smoke and mirrors. Illusions they had clung to. There was no difference between Sebastian and Oliv—Mr. Martin.

Oliver took a deep breath and stepped back. "I thought I was the one nursing a grudge."

Furious with herself, Abigail took a step back. "I shouldn't have come here."

She started to rush past him, but he caught her hand. "John asked me what I wanted to do with the rest of my life. I told him I didn't know. And he said, 'Sometimes a woman can help a man figure out questions like that.'" He pinched his lip and took a deep breath. "I'm not your husband."

Not a plea for her to believe him, but his sincerity frightened her. She heard Mr. Fowler's voice in her head: *"I didn't exactly lie. At one time in his life, Oliver was all those things you're lookin' for in a man. Once upon a time. I thought maybe you'd help him find himself again."*

"I don't want to help you find your answers, Mr. Martin. I've had enough of being the woman a man can lean on, especially when he is drunk, lazy, or just weak." She felt him stiffen and regretted the bite of her words, no matter how true. Their hands slipped away from each other. "Thank you for the money."

Oliver stared out the window at The Angel of Shavano. The snow lying in the gullies and trenches of the distant mountain formed a nearly perfect depiction of a heavenly being. All these months, this was the first time he'd seen it. The light and the snow had to be perfect. He figured the timing was no accident.

"I see the angel, Lord. You telling me that's as close as I'll get to her?"

He swung his gaze toward the door. He hadn't planned on taking John's advice. In fact, Oliver honestly didn't know what caused him to reach out to Abigail like that. And to realize she saw him as weak and floundering—the sting of her words burned him like molten steel.

Couple that with the loss of his best friend and—well, Jubilee Springs had turned about as sour as a town could get.

He hadn't realized how badly he'd wanted Abigail in his life till he saw himself from her perspective, and the view was ugly.

He'd tried so hard not to get hurt, to leave his heart out of this whole mess, and yet, somehow, he'd failed.

Beneath Abigail's low opinion and distrust of him, though, Oliver thought he had glimpsed *something* more. In fact, he was certain of it, but did it amount to a hill of beans? She had her cap set for a business relationship, not a marriage. A Mr. Perfect she could keep at a distance. And it was not possible for Oliver Martin to elevate himself to such a grand—but empty—status. He kicked at a chair leg out of frustration.

Well, regardless, all this was out of his hands and he needed to quit acting like a fool. He was no lovesick schoolboy, he had to make decisions like a man. He was going back to his ranch, to make a go of it, and quit running from life.

"That's what I'll do, Lord. Stop ignoring You and hiding from everything that scares me. Love. Responsibility. Pain. They come whether a man wants them to or not. Fast and merciless. Seems to me the trick is learning to roll with the punches." He glanced over at John's shirt hanging on the hook. "Before I leave, though, I guess I'll tie up a few loose ends."

Well aware he couldn't be more in Abigail's eyes, Oliver did believe he could at least leave her with something to smile about. Maybe she'd even remember his name with fondness when he was done.

CHAPTER 10

"He was supposed to be your husband, wasn't he?" Desi Brinks spun from the shelves behind the mercantile's counter and set the jar of facial cream down in front of Abigail. "'Least that's what I heard?"

"Yes." Abigail had yet to meet anyone in Jubilee Springs with as much enthusiasm for busybodiness as the short, stocky store owner. Kind and friendly, Desi still made every trip to her store a gauntlet of questions for Abigail to run. "How much for the cream?"

"Oh, five cents. You heard about his friend, then?"

"John. Yes." Abigail sifted through her reticule looking for her change purse. "He was kind. I was very sorry to hear the news."

"I hear it has really impacted Oliver. Why, he came in here just yesterday and paid off his account, John's account, and the account for the Madden family."

Abigail swung her head up. "He did? Why the Maddens?" Desi's eyes glittered with excitement. Clearly the woman loved an interested audience for her tidbits of news. "She was widowed, you know. No income. She and her two boys lived just down from Oliver and John."

Abigail was impressed by the gesture, but Desi wasn't done. She tagged Abigail on the hand. "That's not all. He bought her a business to run."

"He did?"

Desi beamed, obviously delighted to deliver news Abigail hadn't heard. "Bought her the leather shop. She can make saddles and such, but eventually she wants to switch over to ladies' fashions."

A little stunned, Abigail handed over a nickel. "My, Oliver—I mean, Mr. Martin—has become quite altruistic."

"He told me he just wants to settle some accounts now that he has the funds."

"Good for him." And Abigail was truly pleased. Perhaps John's death would yield a bumper crop of blessings. She thought the man would like that.

"Oh, and that's the headstone, I bet you."

"What?" Abigail followed the woman's gaze out the window. A wagon rumbled by carrying a piece of white, rectangular marble. Abigail could see writing on it, but could not make out the words. A moment later, Oliver rode by, trailing it.

"Oliver ordered a headstone for John's grave. Taking it up today."

Abigail hoped to go there one day and leave flowers. One day. In the meantime, the man's best friend was seeing to it that the grave would not be lost or forgotten. Oliver's respect and love for John touched Abigail's heart. She had to blink away tears as she watched him ride off.

~

Abigail inked the type, laid the paper in the tympan, lowered it, and rolled the bed in below the platen. Then she grabbed the Devil's Tail and pulled. Over and over and over. In an hour, she had done sixty handbills.

And she hadn't seen one of them.

The mindless, repetitive printing tasks allowed her so much time to think. Too much. She wondered how long she would be able to get away with running Mr. Stewart's shop in his absence. Should she talk to someone about the situation? A lawyer, perhaps? She had hoped to talk to Oliver about it, but felt that bridge was burned.

Oliver.

Deny it all she tried, she still felt his hand on hers, warm and strong. And the tone in his voice when he'd said, *"Sometimes a woman can help a man figure out questions like that."* He'd been probing—not begging—just carefully determining if she might give him a chance.

And she'd run from him.

Abigail still believed she'd done the right thing. She wouldn't ever risk getting involved with the wrong man again.

"Then what is the matter with me?" She slammed down the platen and flinched at the heavy thud. This handbill would not make the grade. She sighed in exasperation.

If I did the right thing, Lord, why can't I let it go? He's all wrong— The bell over the door rang. When she looked up, her heart sank.

Mr. Landers.

She left the press and met him at the counter, intent on keeping him out of the cash register this time. "Can I help you?"

"Stewart's not back, is he?" A little smirk suggested to Abigail that Mr. Landers knew the answer.

"No, sir. I'd be happy to give him a message."

"So, you running the place and pocketing his cash?"

"I am not pocketing anything. Mr. Stewart hired me at a set salary and we have jobs to print. I take my pay and that is all."

Landers's smirk grew. "You're smart as a little fox, aren't you?" He rushed around behind the counter and tried to shove Abigail aside. This time, however, she was ready for him.

Planting her feet, she shoved back, using all the power her small frame could expel. "You are not taking any more of his money until he returns to settle up with you."

The man merely laughed and pushed her aside again. "I'll take what I want and you'll be happy to let me."

He reached into the register and Abigail slammed it shut on his fingers. He howled like an injured wolf, snatching his hand out. His fist reared back as if to strike her and she flinched in anticipation.

"Use that hand against a woman and I'll put a bullet in it."

Oliver!

Abigail was overjoyed to see him standing in the door, a gun in one hand and a picnic basket in the other. Landers scowled and stretched long fingers toward his Colt.

"Pull it and you'll be shaking hands with the devil in the blink of an eye."

The man debated, working his jaw back and forth, but moved his hand away from the weapon. "I liked you better drunk."

"I'm sure you did." Oliver moved to Landers's left. "Step away from her and tell me what's going on here."

"Oliver, please put the gun away."

His eyes widened almost imperceptibly. She had called him Oliver. And he'd caught it.

"I'm not stealing anything," Landers growled. "Stewart owes me some money. A lot of it. I think he's run, which means I can collect anyway I see fit."

"By scaring a woman?"

"My money's in that register."

Oliver shifted to Abigail. "How much of what he says is true?"

Well, her plan had to come apart at some point. *Thank you, Lord, for the money I have saved.* "I think it's all true. Mr. Stewart left me a note saying he was running for his life over a debt. He left my pay in the register. He didn't say he would *never* be back, so I thought I'd just keep working. I take my salary," she glared at Mr. Landers, "and nothing more."

"How much does he owe you, Landers?"

"Oliver, please. The gun. Before someone gets hurt."

He breathed a heavy sigh rich with defeat. After a long hesitation, he holstered his gun, then looked to Landers. "How much?"

Landers tilted his head, surprise on his face. "Two thousand dollars."

Oliver thought it over for a moment, then motioned at the man. "Step outside with me."

"What for?"

"I don't know. Maybe because I holstered my gun and think I can settle this without killing you. I could be wrong."

Landers huffed, but obliged. Oliver raised the basket and handed it off to her. "Thank you for the food."

Abigail clutched it to her and watched the men through the window. The older man gesticulated wildly, and she could hear his raised voice, but not his words. She half-expected Oliver to draw his gun, once out of her sight, but he never did. And after a few moments, Landers calmed, and his tone changed, softened. Oliver patted the air a few times, then finally the two men shook, albeit with a cool indifference.

To her astonishment, they both simply walked away, but in opposite directions.

She was tempted to run after Oliver, find out what had transpired, but pride—or fear—got the better of her.

Until five o'clock.

At which point, overwhelmed by curiosity, she locked the print shop and marched down to his cabin. However, he did not answer several knocks on his door. Frustrated, wondering what, if anything, was afoot, she trudged back to the inn. Her little room struck her as unusually quiet and lonely this evening. Something about twilight always made her feel a touch melancholy anyway. The dying of the light. The inevitable darkness.

Unable to bear it, but not eager for another meal alone in the inn's restaurant, Abigail wandered down to the park on the edge of town. Several couples and a few families were out, strolling, tossing baseballs, enjoying the late August evening. She surveyed the mountains ringing the valley, most snowcapped, turning sapphire and orange in the setting sun. Mt. Shavano touched the sky in the distance, but Abigail couldn't make out the fabled angel.

She settled on a wrought iron bench and breathed in

the fresh air scented with pine. She was glad she'd come here. It soothed her soul. But she wondered what tomorrow would bring. Would Landers be back? Did he have a claim on the print shop? Was she working in vain?

Oh, Lord, I so need Your direction now. I miss James and Artemus almost more than I can bear. I just want them with me.

She imagined them on the grassy opening, playing catch, laughing, and the game devolving into a wrestling match. Spirited boys, they would do well out West.

"A pretty flower for a pretty lady." Startled, Abigail looked up into a stranger's face.

A handsome young man with dark hair, dark eyes, and a stunning smile presented Abigail with a red rose. "You look like you need cheering up."

"Uh, well," flustered, she took the flower. "Yes, thank you. You're very kind."

He offered his hand. "I'm William Blakely. And we've met."

"Abigail Holt. We have?"

"I was coming out of the telegraph office. You were going in."

"Ah." Abigail bit down a smile. "I do remember."

He took a step back after the handshake, opening up a respectable distance between them. "I'm the corporate attorney for Bannister Holdings out of New York. At least, I will be. Official at eight o'clock tomorrow when I move into my office."

"Oh, you are new."

"Yes." He laughed and shoved his hands into his pockets. "Have you lived in Jubilee Springs long? What do you think of it? I've only spoken to mine management and I'm sure they want me to have a"—he glanced at the flower—"rosy picture of the town. Someone else's perspective might be helpful. The mayor and a few others want me to bring in investors."

"I have been here almost a month. It seems to be a nice, prosperous town." He was a pleasant enough sort of fellow, mannerly and handsome. Dressed impeccably in a tailored linen suit. Remembering her own manners, she motioned to the bench. "Please have a seat."

"I wouldn't want to intrude. You looked lost in deep contemplation."

"A respite from my musings would be welcome."

He nodded and sat at the other end of the bench. "You're new in town, as well then. What brings you to Jubilee Springs? If I'm not being too inquisitive."

"No, no." Abigail decided to skip over the mail-order bride chapter and simplify her story. "I work at the print shop. I'm a recent widow. I relocated due to my husband's death."

"I am so terribly sorry for your loss."

"Thank you." She did not miss Sebastian, but she had never wished death on him, especially knowing he was lost in his sin. "I have two young sons and hope to bring them out here soon. I think they'll like it." She certainly adored the temperatures. Atlanta in August felt like a sopping wet towel draped over your shoulders. The mild days and cool evenings here suited Abigail perfectly.

"Where are your children now?"

"A boarding school in Atlanta."

"Ah, a roommate of mine at Harvard hailed from Atlanta. I thought I recognized the accent."

"You are from…?"

"Massachusetts. Son of a minister. In fact, my father is

contemplating starting a church over in Monarch Bend. Just a few miles away. We are Baptists."

"I'm a Methodist. There is a community church in town, but I haven't attended yet."

"I won't hold that against you."

"Which one? That I'm a Methodist or that I haven't attended church yet?"

They laughed again and Abigail was glad that she'd met Mr. Blakely. Chatting with a friend at least held off the loneliness of twilight a bit longer.

"I may encourage my brother to relocate here, but it remains to be seen. He owns a mercantile back in Boston. He'd have to decide if he should sell it or move the business here."

"Oh, well, I know there is a mercantile in town, but Jubilee Springs may be big enough for two."

"I'll be looking into it." He slapped his knees. "Well, I suppose I should be heading back. Can I escort you somewhere?"

They both rose. "I'm staying at the River Valley Inn."

"What happy fortune. As am I." Mr. Blakely offered his elbow. "I wonder, Mrs. Holt...I don't drink, but could I entice you to join me for coffee?"

Suddenly, Abigail realized Mr. Blakely was all but shouting his qualifications from the rooftops, whether intentionally or not. "Mr. Blakely, why did you give me this flower?"

His eyebrows rose. "I saw you sitting here. They were growing on the fence." He shrugged. "I apologize if it was forward of me. Normally, I am not so bold, but honestly, Mrs. Holt, you looked like you needed a friend. And as I am unattached at the moment"—the corner of his mouth turned up—"I saw no harm in the gesture."

"Well, thank you, Mr. Blakely. I appreciate your honesty and your boldness. Yes, a hot cup of coffee sounds inviting."

Linking her arm with his, Abigail accepted the fact that Mr. Blakely was not Oliver, but he *was* imminently more qualified. Not that Oliver had anything at all to do with her choices. The unbidden comparison was annoying and pointless. "Tell me, Mr. Blakely, do you have any other siblings?"

"No, only a nephew and a niece much younger than I. Twelve and fourteen. I miss them terribly."

"You like children? Or just your family?"

"I will admit a deep, unabashed love of children. Their laughter lifts my spirits. Any age. They all have something unique that makes me smile."

As they headed back toward town, Abigail pondered Mr. Blakely and how perfect he was—on the surface.

Did You bring me here for him, Lord? Is he the man I should have met? But what of the print shop and the newspaper?

*Or Oliver...*the thought echoed in her mind.

Stop it, Abigail. You just met the man. Don't be ridiculous.

Frustrated, she reminded herself she had come to Jubilee Springs originally as a way to find a father for her children and to avoid a menial, poverty-stricken existence. She would keep her focus on her work at the print shop—she sneaked a glance at Mr. Blakely—and consider carefully, harshly, any other options that might present themselves.

~

"Oliver, it's getting late and I would like to close up."

Oliver finished buttoning his new shirt and stepped out of the mercantile's changing closet.

Mr. Brinks whistled in apparent astonishment. "Well, I'll be. Oliver, you're a new man. Haircut, a shave, new clothes. What's come over you?"

He plucked his cowboy hat from a nearby table, started to put it on, but paused. Dingy, sweat-stained, it showed its age. "I'll need a new hat, too." He looked up. "To answer your question, John was expecting more from me. I owe it to him. And God took me straight to that nugget. A man would be a fool to ignore a blessing like that. I'm no fool. Not anymore."

The old gentleman folded his arms across his chest and tilted his head. "John always told me there was more to you than what this town was seeing. I'm glad to know he was right." Mr. Brinks extended his hand. "I believe you'll do him proud."

Oliver slipped on his new hat and strode down the boardwalk. Evening was falling. Long shadows crept across the street. The traffic had thinned out considerably and the town was quieting. This used to be his favorite time of day.

Back on the ranch, he and John had developed a habit of sitting a spell on the porch just after dinner. Digesting and resting, as he used to say. Then they'd make plans, everything from the next day's herd movements to what structures they might want to build. They'd continued the tradition here in Jubilee Springs…

Until his death, of course. Now, Oliver had the evenings to himself, but he continued the tradition, in a manner anyway. He would sit alone and plan. He had set the wheels in motion on a few things. He'd finish up here and head back to the ranch sometime in the next several days. He'd decided he would sell the claim where the nugget was found and stick to ranching.

As he wandered past a restaurant, a patron exited, and a woman's laughter followed on the cooler, coffee-scented air. The sound was light and almost magical. Oliver knew the voice, of course.

Could he join her? On the other hand, why bother? Her mind was made up about him.

Still, the urge to glance over would not be denied. Through the window, he spotted Abigail sipping coffee, smiling...and chatting with a man.

Oliver stopped, taken aback, not at the sight of the handsome gentleman wearing nice clothes, sporting clean hands and good manners. But at the smile on Abigail's face. A lightning bolt of jealousy whipped through him, but it almost instantly dissolved into disappointment.

Well, he knew there was great potential for this plan to backfire. She had met William Blakely—Mr. Perfect. And he did look to suit her.

More bitter than he knew he had a right to be, he shook his head. He had no claim on the woman. She'd made that abundantly clear.

Seeing her with the man settled at least one issue in his mind. Mr. Perfect would win in a head-to-head competition. So, Oliver had one last task, and then he was leaving Jubilee Springs in the dust.

CHAPTER 11

Abigail stepped into the hallway, closed her door behind her, and turned to lock it. Three days. Three days had passed with no sign of Oliver and no repeat visit to the print shop by Mr. Landers. Had Oliver somehow talked the man into letting the debt go? She desperately wanted to know but hadn't been able to bring herself to make another trip to his cabin.

Because she wanted him to come see her. She was a proud fool. If he didn't come by today, though—

She slid the key into the lock, but a closing door at the end of the hall drew her attention.

"Mrs. Holt." Mr. Blakely locked his door and strode down to her, impeccably dressed, every hair in place. His normal state of affairs, she guessed. "I was hoping I would run into you today. My new position has kept me very busy these last few days—getting acclimated to things and whatnot, but I was, uh, wondering..." He cleared his throat. "Well, I enjoyed our chat the other evening. I was wondering if you might join me for dinner tonight."

Abigail tried to ignore the puzzling, sinking feeling his request elicited in her. She had no reason to feel this way. Pursuing the better part of wisdom, or so she argued, she smiled. "Yes, thank you for asking. I'd enjoy that."

And Abigail *did* enjoy Mr. Blakely's company. She ambled down Main Street, contemplating his qualifications. He came from a respectable home. He exhibited impeccable manners. He was educated, intelligent, conversational. He enjoyed children. She'd seen no evidence of a temper or affinity for alcohol.

Yet, somehow, he left her feeling a touch...empty. Or at least something that couldn't be described as happy. Truthfully, she didn't know the right word.

Lost in thought, she was surprised to find herself so quickly at the front door of the print shop. She took a deep breath and forced herself to focus. She unlocked the door and let herself in, but wound up pausing at the counter, her gaze roaming over the business.

How much more effort should she put into the shop? Was this any kind of a plan? Keep working until the owner came back? What if he never did?

"Business that bad?"

She whirled around. "Oliver. I mean, Mr. Martin." She hadn't even heard the bell.

He bounced his hat in his hands and smiled sheepishly. "You can stick with Oliver."

She started to ask his business, but stopped. He had shaved again. Dark hair, now neatly trimmed and tucked behind his ear, revealed a slight scar at his temple. Most impressive, however, were the new, *pressed* clothes he wore. Tan pants, black suspenders, glistening boots, and a spotless white shirt bespoke the change she had sensed previously. Every time she saw him now, he seemed to be improving.

She was glad for him. He clearly was not standing still any longer. She wondered, too, if now she would know what had resulted from his chat with Mr. Landers. "What can I help you with, Mr. Martin?" She sounded a touch too cold and formal, but wasn't that best?

"I came by to give you this." He pulled a wrinkled note from his pocket and handed it to her.

Curious, Abigail unfolded it. Scrawled handwriting said, *I, Clem Stewart, owe Jim Landers twenty-two hundred dollars.* Below that, the handwriting changed and read, *Paid in full. Jim Landers.*

Questions raced by in her mind. "I don't understand. Is Mr. Stewart back? He's paid his debt to this man? He'll be coming back to the print shop?"

"Stewart is not back. What this piece of paper means is that Landers can't come in here and demand any more money from you. If he tries, tell me or the sheriff."

"Yes. All right." Unsure what this meant to her position at the paper, she trudged over to the cash register and slipped it under the drawer for safekeeping.

"You don't look happy. I thought you'd be glad to know Landers wouldn't be bothering you again."

She was glad, but how had this come about? "Did you pay Mr. Stewart's debt?"

"Yes. It's my intention to right some wrongs before I leave town."

"I've heard—wait. You're leaving?" She hated the disappointment that rose in her voice. "Where are you going?" *Why* was he leaving? Could he be running from her? She shouldn't flatter herself, but the question gained in importance. "Why did you pay his debt?"

"I thought it might bring you some peace of mind. Landers can be intimidating to most folks."

"You did this for me?" *Please say yes.*

He didn't respond immediately, then only shrugged a shoulder, an almost imperceptible motion.

"Thank you." Gratitude thawed some of her resistance to him. She could feel it draining away, but they couldn't let this moment go on. "I've heard about your good deeds around town. And I saw, in passing, the headstone. Someday I'd like to leave flowers at John's grave."

"You would?"

"Yes, I would."

As he stared at her with open longing, Abigail feared the dangerous, unspoken emotions swirling between them. *They have to stay unspoken—especially now that you are leaving, Oliver.*

They could not dance any closer to this flame. She wouldn't survive another drunken, violent, lying husband. Nor would she put her children through such again, even though she doubted Oliver was anything like Sebastian.

And that doubt stalked her resistance.

Aware they had inadvertently drawn a little closer, Abigail literally took a step back and tried to turn the conversation away from her heart. "Oliver, regarding Mr. Stewart's debt, I have a related question."

For an instant, a shadow of disappointment tugged at his face, but he passed it off. Smiling, he laid his hat on the counter and nodded. "Shoot."

"Umm, well, as I said earlier, I had thought I would continue to work here, keep the print shop running, pay the bills, collect my pay—and only the pay I'm entitled to—and save the money for Mr. Stewart."

"But I get the impression he isn't coming back."

"He could change his mind. I want his business to be here for him and..."

"And?"

"I don't want to look for another position. I like working in the print shop. My father owned one."

"All right." Oliver rubbed his jaw, pondering. "So what's your question?"

Her turn to shrug. "Is it a terrible idea, running his business in his absence, telling customers he'll be back? Am I a thief? A liar? Both?"

Oliver huffed a long breath. "If you're not taking money you're not entitled to, you're not a thief. As to the liar part, do you think he'll be back?"

"I don't know. I don't know Mr. Stewart well enough to really make an educated guess."

"I know him. He's not beyond making some bad choices and running with some questionable company." He paused here. "But if you keep his shop up and running and then he comes back, who's to say he won't do the same dumb thing again? He likes to play cards. Only, what if he gambles the shop away next time?"

Abigail had thought of that. The whole thing was a gamble. "I was willing to risk it."

"For how long?"

"I don't understand."

"What if he comes back in two years? Five even? You've

invested all this hard work in the shop, and he'll just waltz in and claim ownership?"

"It's his shop."

"Yeah, maybe."

"You think it's not?"

"I think there is such a thing as abandonment. Applies to gold claims. Maybe it would apply to a business."

"I'm not sure I'd feel right about just taking his business."

"It's not taking it if he's really abandoned it. You need a lawyer."

Abigail snapped her fingers. "Mr. Blakely."

Mr. Martin pulled back ever-so-slightly. "Blakely?"

"He is a corporate attorney, here for a holding company looking into business with the town."

Abigail wasn't sure, but she thought she saw a hint of dismay on Oliver's face. "That the fella you had dinner with the other night?"

"I haven't had dinner with him yet." She paused. He'd seen her? "We were having coffee."

Oliver tapped his fingers on the counter. "Nice fella?"

"Yes, I believe so."

"Gonna marry him?"

"That's hardly an appropriate question. And I barely know him."

"Do his qualifications suit?"

A little frustrated with this line of questioning, Abigail huffed a breath and raised her hands to her hips. "This is not relevant at all to what we were just discussing."

"But you were in such an all-fired hurry to marry a man with good qualifications when you got here. What's changed? His aren't good enough either?"

"I will tell you what's changed and why I want to keep my position here at the print shop. Time. With employment, I have time to..."

"Shop around?"

She glared at him. "Or not at all. It's my choice. I'm not desperate."

"So, when you were desperate, I still wasn't good enough?"

Her mouth fell open. Their gazes locked. Why was he being so petulant? Especially since he was leaving. "Are you still angry with me over my desire to marry a sober and wise man?"

Oliver's shoulders sagged a little. Abigail thought she had humbled him some, but wondered why they were even having this conversation.

"Would you say you're looking at men with fresh eyes now?"

Not sure of the answer he expected, she thought about the question and nodded. "Yes. Perhaps my expectations were too high. I just want a man who is good and kind, and who will love me and my children."

"Thought you didn't want love to enter into it."

She froze. *Yes, when had that changed, Lord?* Though the answer stared her in the face, she didn't want to see it.

"You'll find him if you keep looking."

Though he said it rather matter-of-factly, she couldn't help but think there was some message behind his words.

"It's not my area, but honestly, I would urge you to be cautious, Abigail." Gentle chatter and the clink of dinnerware surrounded Abigail's conversation with Mr. Blakely here in the restaurant. He sliced into his steak and shook his head. "Mr. Stewart could argue he never intended to abandon the business. You'd have to prove his intent."

"Because he didn't specifically say, in the note, he was abandoning the business?"

"Exactly."

While she had suspected as much, *her* intent had never been to claim the print shop. "I just want a job. I want to work so I can bring James and Artemus out here and take care of them." She laid down her own fork. The meal was no longer all that appetizing.

Mr. Blakely wiped his lips with his napkin and set down his own fork, a piece of steak on it. "Abigail, your intentions were good and pure. You've done nothing wrong. But you should protect yourself. If Mr. Stewart returns and takes over again, I wouldn't want him trying to claim you've embezzled funds—"

"Embezzled?" she squeaked, drawing curious glances from a nearby table. She lowered her voice. "I haven't embezzled anything. I've been meticulous with the books."

"Yes, but he could claim you didn't write everything down."

"Why would he do that?"

"If he is a man of low character, to force you into giving back your wages."

Stunned, Abigail sat back in her chair. "I just wanted to keep working."

"A noble endeavor."

Abigail could feel Mr. Blakely's gaze searching her face, but she didn't want to look at him. At this moment, she just wanted to sit in a corner and cry.

"Abigail," he reached out and placed his hand atop hers.

Oddly, she saw Oliver in his cabin, the glow of sunset surrounding him. The longing in his face when he'd pulled her to her feet. Where would she be now if he'd kissed her?

"Abigail, I wanted to tell you that I am immensely impressed by your courage. Coming out here alone to seek a future for you and your family. You're very brave. And I should confess to you that I asked around about you. I know you came out here as a mail-order bride."

Her cheeks flushed. "Yes, I did."

"May I ask what happened?"

What *had* happened to Oliver? Quite a bit in a few short weeks. "The groom, Oliver Martin, wasn't…ready." What? Where had that come from? Wasn't the word *acceptable*? For some reason, she hated to say that. It struck her as judgmental now. "I mean, he wasn't…" She brushed a stray hair off her forehead and licked her lips. "He wasn't, um, I mean, the truth of it is he wasn't expecting me." Humiliating to admit, but surely most people in Jubilee Springs had figured it out by now.

"You came all this way to marry him and he had no idea?"

"None. He didn't want to get married, and I didn't want to marry him."

"You mean after you met him? Why was that?"

"I had a list of qualifications I was intent on my groom meet. Mr. Martin did not meet them…then."

"Then. Has something changed? Have you changed your mind about him?"

"No." Had she? The answer felt, well, not like a lie exactly. "I think he was going through a difficult time when

I arrived. I think the shock of losing his best friend brought him back around to the man he was."

"So would you consider marrying him now?"

"No! Goodness, no. I would…I would…" she faded off, troubled by something in her answers. "Why are you asking me all these questions?"

"I saw Mr. Martin yesterday. Or more precisely, I overheard him. He paid off Stewart's gambling debt and told Landers not to bother you anymore. I thought that was interesting. He was rather *forceful* in his declaration."

The gesture had certainly touched Abigail. Had her warring in her mind and heart. "Yes, I know."

"Anyway, it got me to wondering what you might be thinking of him." Mr. Blakely slid his other hand over and grasped hers. Startled, she looked up into his longing gaze. "The man was a fool for ever letting you slip away."

"Thank you, but—"

"I would have done whatever it took to win you."

"My list of qualifications was a bit unrealistic, I suppose."

"How do I measure up?"

Abigail held her breath. He was perfect. "I think if I had met you when I arrived instead of Oliver…" She looked out the window. Different. Everything would have been different. "I would have made a terrible mistake."

Oliver moseyed up to Blakely, who was cinching the saddle on a rental horse, and leaned on the sorrel's rear end. "I got your note. You wanted to see me?"

The man smiled up at him from beneath his black

Stetson as he reached beneath the horse. "Oliver Martin, you are one big fool."

"So I've been told. That's not new information."

When Oliver met Blakely in the Assayer's Office and they'd had a friendly conversation, he'd realized the man was perfect for Abigail. After returning to town with the nugget, Oliver explained to him Abigail's plan to marry the most qualified man and not be entangled emotionally. Oliver then encouraged Blakely to introduce himself. The recommendation had cut Oliver to the core, but he wanted Abigail to be happy.

Blakely had agreed eagerly, pointing out that he was always happy to dine with a lovely lady. If more came of it, he wouldn't fight destiny.

Oliver harbored a secret hope, however, that Abigail might decide perfection wasn't what she wanted after all. The plan had been a dangerous gamble. High stakes indeed.

Blakely threaded the cinch and buckled it. Satisfied the saddle was in place, he stood up, eye to eye with Oliver. "I may be perfect for the young lady as you suggested, but I don't believe she couldn't care less. I would take it personally, if it wasn't obvious she has eyes for someone else."

"Someone else?"

Blakely snorted then swung up into the saddle, barely missing Oliver's head with a boot heel. "She can talk qualifications and perfection all she wants, but what she really wants is to marry for love." He winked at Oliver. "One day, I might tell her what you tried to give her." He spun the horse and pointed it out of town. "A magnanimous, selfless gesture on your part. However, the lady and I are not meant for each other. Go win the fair maiden's hand."

Laughing, Blakely nudged his horse to a trot and headed out.

Oliver was a bit stunned. Could he yet win the lady's hand? What should he do?

Maybe he'd already done it.

He glanced up at Blakey disappearing down Main Street.

Time would tell, he supposed. Time would tell.

CHAPTER 12

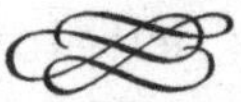

Abigail's blood froze in her veins as she read the telegram again.

Children are gone. Per your request, released to your legal representative four days ago.

Per my request? My representative?

There must be some mistake. None of this made any sense. Who would take her children?

She felt faint.

"Ma'am," the clerk asked carefully, "you all right? You're white as milk."

"I need to send another telegram. I need—I need to know where my children are." Abigail reached for the pencil with shaking hands and scribbled furiously. She checked on James and Artemus once a week. They had not mentioned anything in their responses or the one letter they'd written about any relatives. She slid the paper back to the clerk. "Please send this immediately."

Oh, God, where are they?

She wanted help. She wanted comfort. She wanted Oliver. Somehow, she knew he could steady her.

She started down the boardwalk at a fast pace, but it quickly turned into a run. *Oh, Lord, please help me find my children. Please let them be all right. Help me find Oliver.* She ignored the questioning stares as she raced down the boardwalk. Had Oliver left town already? Surely he wouldn't without saying goodbye. He couldn't go. At least not yet.

Wiping tears from her eyes, she stepped down to cross Telegraph Street, headed toward his cabin on the edge of town—

"Momma!"

Abigail skidded to a stop and turned to the crowd on the walk. Heart pounding in her ears, she wondered if panic and desperation had spawned illusions in her mind.

"Ma!"

Yes, that was James! "James! Artemus!" She frantically searched the human wave of plaid and leather, bobbing parasols, fluttering skirts, and strange faces flowing down the boardwalk. Suddenly, her boys crashed through the wall of people and leaped into her arms, nearly knocking her over.

Joy, wide, deep, breathtaking, filled her soul as she wrapped her angels in her arms. *Oh, God, thank You, thank You, thank You—*

She and her boys laughed, cried, and hugged so tightly she thought bones might break. "I don't understand," she said through tears, "Why—how are you here?" She squeezed the two giggling boys harder. "Not that I care. I don't care. You're here and that's all that matters."

"We missed you, Ma." James buried his round face in her shoulder and tried to hide his tears.

"We did, Momma, terrible," Artemus chimed in.

That was when she looked over the top of their heads and saw Oliver smiling at them. And she knew. His good deeds. Thank God for his good deeds. She closed her eyes and hugged her boys fiercely.

When their laughter faded and her senses returned, Abigail wiped her face and knelt in the dust on the side of the street. She held her boys at arm's length and surveyed them top to bottom. They were dusty, wearing clothes wrinkled from the three-day train ride, and their hair needed combing badly. Their cheeks were a bit pale, as well, but they were the most beautiful things she had ever seen.

"Oh, boys, I can't tell you how much it means to have you here with me. How I have missed you." She couldn't resist one last hug, then backed off to let them breathe.

"The man who met us at the station, Ma, is he your new husband?" James lifted his chin like a skeptical young man ready for information he didn't necessarily want.

Abigail touched his cheek. "Um, no. No, he's not. He didn't quite…I mean, he wasn't…I have a fine job, and in time I might remarry. We'll see where the Lord leads." She looked over their shoulders again, but Oliver was gone. Fear struck her. Sudden and jarring. He couldn't leave, at least not until Abigail said some things he was entitled to hear.

"I liked that man," Artemus said, scanning the town with his usual curious eye. "Every time he said your name, his voice got kind of soft. Does this town have an ice cream parlor?"

“That’s true,” James agreed. “And we are hungry. Can we eat?”

“I like him, too,” Abigail said softly. Emotions raged in her heart. She had to see him. “I tell you what, boys, I’ll take you back to the hotel. Get you dinner there and then meet you back in our room. I need to run an errand. That nice man who brought you here—” Her throat tightened and she swallowed against the knot. “That nice man is leaving town, and I have to thank him for bringing you here.”

“He said you’d be surprised.” Artemus chuckled. “I thought you were gonna faint dead away in the street.”

“I nearly did.” She ruffled his dark hair.

“Oh, heck, I almost forgot.” James reached inside his coat and pulled out an envelope. “He told me to give you this.”

Abigail wasn’t sure she could take another shock today. With a trembling hand, she opened the envelope. Inside, she found a bill of sale. Signed by Mr. Stewart.

The print shop was hers.

Oliver shoved a shirt into his saddle bag, but his mind drifted back to the street. That one reunion had almost made the pain of losing John worth it. He wished his old friend could have seen Abigail with her boys. A knot tried to tie itself up in Oliver’s throat and he swallowed. Maybe he’d finally done some good. Not that it mattered. He shook his head and shoved another shirt into his bag. A shadow filled his open doorway and he looked up.

Sunset glowed behind Abigail, outlining her hourglass figure in a perfect silhouette. “Oliver.” Her voice shook something loose in him and his knees turned to water. He had to remind himself to breathe. She was here. Should he hope this was more than a goodbye?

She stepped slowly into the cabin, and the amber light shimmered in her hair, highlighted soft, flawless skin, and gleamed in her eyes. She took his breath away. Leaving her would be the hardest thing he'd ever done in his life…and the most necessary, if he ever wanted to get *on* with his life.

"You weren't going to leave without saying goodbye, were you?"

Was he? "You've got your boys. You won't miss me."

She crossed the floor to him. "Oliver, I don't have the words to thank you."

He swallowed and looked away. Those mesmerizing eyes of hers, skin as soft and pure as a fresh peach, begged for his touch, and to possess that mouth…he couldn't think. "It was nothing. I just wanted you to…be happy."

"In eleven years of marriage, my husband never once said those words to me. Not once." She took a step closer. "How did you get my boys here? How did you get the print shop?"

"Well, for the first, I lied and sent the school a telegram under your name. A Pinkerton picked up James and Artemus and escorted them here. The Pinkertons also found Stewart for me."

He couldn't help it. He let his gaze drift back to her. One kiss. Could he live off one kiss for the rest of his life? As if under a spell, his hand came up and cupped her cheek.

"I don't want you—" Her chin quivered. She frowned, tried again. "I don't want you to leave us, Oliver. I think you are a good man. You—" Her lips moved as she searched for the words, but no sound came out. She shook her head. "I don't even know what I'm trying to say. I've never felt this way before, not even with Sebastian. Can I be in love with you?"

The question startled him. *Was* this love? He'd attached all kinds of emotions to it, wondered why she affected him the way she did. Had he been dancing around the truth just because he was too gun-shy to label it? "I'd marry you, Abigail. Would you marry me? I don't mean would you marry me. I mean, would you marry me now if you were still of a mind to be a bride? Do I meet your qualifications?"

She smiled and laid her hand over his, still on her cheek. "You exceed them. I'm ashamed I ever even tried to qualify a man like you. And, yes, I would marry you."

Silence fell. What were they saying? "I'm not like Sebastian. You believe that?"

"Yes. And I'm not like Avonia. You believe that?"

He encircled her, drew her against him, hardly able to believe he had her in his arms. She tilted her face up and he pressed his lips to hers. Desire raced through his body like an out-of-control prairie blaze, but at the same time... peace washed over him.

Abigail wrapped her arms around his neck and pulled him closer. They deepened the kiss, and Oliver nearly did stop breathing. He heard her give the softest moan. The sound ignited flames in his soul, but the fire was far richer and deeper than physical passion. He ran his hands through her hair, imagining it all loose on the pillow next to him...and in the rocking chair beside him years from now.

"I sure didn't expect to fall into this," he whispered

against the softness of her forehead. "Abigail, I don't want to leave you. And I could marry you today, if you'd have me...but I would like to court you first." He pulled back and cupped her cheeks. John had told him to take that one piece of advice. "You deserve...you deserve to be cherished. Honored." Oliver could hardly believe he was saying these things, but Abigail was a priceless treasure, and he wanted her to know it. She had to trust him. Believe in him. "I want to prove to you—to me—I'm the man...I'm the man you deserve."

Abigail sniffed and blinked back tears from her eyes. "You already have."

He leaned down and kissed her again, lost in love, overwhelmed with peace, happy that the man he was had come back around...thanks to God and a meddlesome best friend.

THE TRUE STORY OF OLIVER

THE FACTS BEHIND THE FICTION

And now, as Paul Harvey used to say, here's the rest of the story.

Oliver Martin and John Fowler were indeed best friends. Oliver was a good-for-nothing slacker who didn't even own a pan. History says his friend John wasn't much better. The two knocked around California gold towns such as El Dorado and Yuba, panning, drinking, doing odd jobs, but mostly, drinking.

On the night of November 7, 1854, the two were meandering drunkenly from one mining camp to the next when a storm hit. They managed to hole up in an abandoned miner's shack on Grizzly Mountain.

They couldn't have picked a worse spot.

The peculiarly heavy rain triggered a flash flood, and a sudden, roaring wall of water hit the cabin, washing both men downriver. Oliver managed to lodge himself in a stand of oak trees till morning. John was not so fortunate.

The next day, Oliver was obliged to bury his friend. He had not dug down two feet when he found a nugget of gold that weighed in at over *eighty-five* pounds. One of the largest ever found in California. Oliver sold it for nearly $650,000—in twenty-first-century dollars.

The nugget made him more than rich. It made him responsible. Convinced the Almighty expected him to do something with his life, Oliver sobered up, invested in various mining businesses, became a philanthropic citizen, and died in New Orleans, a millionaire several times over.

I include this story in case anyone wants to imply my tale is a bit unbelievable. All I can say is, God thought of it first.

Thank you for reading *A Good Man Comes Around.* Eventually, most of them do.

A SNEAK PEEK AT: HANG YOUR HEART ON CHRISTMAS

THE BRIDES OF EVERGREEN BOOK ONE

CHAPTER 1

US Marshal Robert *Dent* Hernandez signed the voucher and slid it back across the desk to the sheriff. "That'll do it." *Two down...how many more to go?*

Sheriff Ben Hayes leaned back in his chair and regarded Dent with that familiar, pitying expression. "Son, aren't you tired?"

Dent held his breath to keep from sighing. Ben, with his barrel chest and graying hair, was a good man, but he was too eager to share his thirty years of lawman wisdom. "No, sir." Dent swiped his hat up off the desk. "Bringin' 'em in is my job."

"You know that's not what I'm talkin' about. Your pa wouldn't want you throwing your life away on his account."

Dent dropped his hat on his head. "If the men I arrest don't have a chance to kill somebody else's pa, that's not a waste." He touched the brim in goodbye. "I'm gonna go get some lunch. I'll head out with the prisoners after."

He stepped out on the now-sun-washed main street of

Evergreen and flinched at the mud. Six straight days of autumn rains had turned the normally dusty street into a quagmire. Off to his left, four men, covered head to toe in the muck, sweated and cursed the mess as they worked to pry their wagon loose. Mules strained and tugged. The sucking sound from the wheels drowned out the noise from the rest of the mud-weary traffic.

"Dent," Ben stepped up beside him, "you don't take a day off. You don't rest. You swing through town once in a blue moon, and then you're gone again. You got roots in this town and they're dying."

"That would be a tragedy."

"You could attend a dance every now and then." Ben wiggled his eyebrows. "Git your arms around a pretty girl. Bid on a sweet apple pie."

Dent didn't care to reply. He continued watching the men mired in the mud. *Most excitement this town has seen in a decade.*

"That hate's gonna eat you up, son. One day you'll wake up fat, old, and alone—like me—and wonder what it was all for."

That last part surprised Dent. "You're a good lawman, Ben. You don't think it's been worth it? Think about who you've helped put in jail."

Ben sighed and swiped his hand over his face. "You're missing my point. You can do your job and have a life, too. I know that now. I didn't when your pa and I were young."

The fire that burned in Dent's belly didn't agree. One day, he would get the final clue. One day, he would arrest the men who had shot his father. He could wait. He could be patient. He could not, however, waste time attending dances and sampling pies. "I thank you for your advice, Ben. You know I respect your opinion."

Ben laid a hand on Dent's shoulder, a breeze stirring his faded brown hair. "Say the word, and you can be my deputy any time."

He bit back a derisive snort. Evergreen, a nice, quiet town, was just the place for a middle-aged lawman tired of chasing criminals. Nearing thirty, Dent was *not* middle-aged or tired. "Well, I thank you for the offer. And I will consider it."

"Yeah, sure you will." Ben squeezed his shoulder and went back inside.

At the depot, Dent tugged at the shackles on his prisoners, hands then feet, then stepped back to stand beside Ben. The two lawmen appraised the offenders. *Happy* Jack Briscomb—short, stocky, face bruised from tripping over Dent's fist—scowled like he was anything *but* happy. His comrade, Needles Jones, a slender, dark-haired fella with one wayward eye, glared at them as he defiantly clanked the shackles at his wrists.

Ben tagged Dent in the ribs. "Watch him," he said, motioning to Needles. "He's got a bad temper…why he's in trouble in the first place."

"Will do." Dent walked around behind the men and gave them a nudge. "All right, boys, here comes the train." The two shuffled over to the edge of the platform. The deafening chug-chug-chug drowned out any further conversation as they waited for the crawling iron horse to enter the station. Amid the hiss and steam and an ear-splitting whistle, the *Cheyenne to Lander* slowed and halted.

The conductor jumped down and set the step in place for the passengers. One by one, dusty cowboys, slick salesmen in cheap suits, and harried mothers battling defiant toddlers emerged from the train. Some embraced their loved ones. Others disappeared into the swirl of bodies. Dent's gaze darted all around, looking for trouble, intent on preventing his charges from getting any stupid ideas. Trouble could always come anytime, anywhere, from fellas like these. He doubted whether the folks of Evergreen could take the shock.

When a lull in the debarking hit, he shook Hayes's hand. "I'll try to stay longer my next time through."

"I'll hold you to it."

Dent pushed his prisoners forward, but had to wait again as a green cotton dress flitted down the steps. "Pardon us, ma'am," he said, pulling Happy and Needles back by their collars.

He couldn't help but notice the dress was filled nicely with a pretty, young gal, wearing silver-rimmed glasses. Thick, wavy, auburn hair, held partially in a barrette, hung at her shoulders, wispy curls framed a sweet, but intelligent, face.

Her eyes, a sparkling, mesmerizing blue, passed over the men, then suddenly widened with stark terror. In a blur of motion, Needles reached back and clawed for Dent's gun. Dent felt the revolver slipping from his holster and grabbed for it. His grip was awkward at best, obstructed by his prisoner's chains and handcuffs.

Needles jerked the gun free, spun, and fired. The young lady and the women nearby screamed, men gasped. Folks scrambled for cover. Somehow, the shot missed Dent. Needles, reacting as fast as a riled snake, draped his shackled arms over the terrified woman. Dent moved to lunge. The outlaw clutched the woman tighter and stepped back with her, shaking his head. He raised the revolver and cocked the hammer.

Dent clenched his jaw and stilled.

The young lady paled to the pallor of chalk dust and appeared to quit breathing.

"You ain't hanging me, lawdog." Needles splayed one hand over the girl's midsection. His filthy fingers caressed her ribs. "Now git me a horse or I'm gonna drop her."

A deep, black, slithering hate rose up in Dent as he evaluated the outlaw. A greasy creature, he was just the sort who would shoot a woman. He was here now because he'd snapped and shot a blacksmith in Topeka. Unpredictable with that temper of his.

"Hey, hey, hey." Happy threw his shackled hands in the air and took two steps away from the fracas. "I don't want no part of this, Marshal. I ain't in on it." He swiveled to Needles. "You don't know what you've done. You don't know who he is."

Grinning, Needles pushed the barrel of the gun into the cleft between the woman's breasts, eliciting a whimper from her. "Ask me if I care. Git me a horse, Marshal. I'll leave the lady and ride out. No harm done."

The woman's eyes spoke volumes. *Save me, please,* she implored silently. He noted absently that her peril should affect him. But all he cared about was how the next few seconds were going to play out.

He flicked his wrist, and the Derringer slid into his hand. His arm shot out like a lightning bolt and he squeezed the trigger. Needles's head jerked with the report of the gun. Blood and brain matter exploded out the back of his head. The lady screamed, her eyes rolled back in her head, and both she and the outlaw hit the ground.

"Dent," Ben's labored, breathless voice came from behind.

Keeping his gun pointed at Needles, Dent glanced back, then looked again. Blood gushed from Ben's chest. His gaze bored into Dent as he reached out. "Sorry, son...I wish I'd..." Ben's knees buckled.

Dent rushed to him, heedless of Needles or the woman. "No, Ben," he caught his friend as he pitched forward. *No, not Ben...*

CHAPTER 2

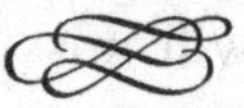

Dent wouldn't have thought it possible that such a catastrophe could unfold in Evergreen, of all places. If only he hadn't been distracted, for the breath of an instant, by shimmering, blue eyes.

Sick over his costly stupidity, he pinched the bridge of his nose and dropped down into a chair at Doc Woodruff's office. Somehow, in one terrible, swift moment, he'd shot his prisoner dead, scared an innocent bystander out of her wits...and lost the man who had been a second father to him.

The shot still rang in his ears

He touched the blood-soaked bib of his shirt, incredulous.

Ben was dead.

At least, so was Needles. Good riddance.

Dent struggled with the way his grief gave way too easily to the thirst for revenge. He couldn't arrest them all, but he had made another permanent dent in the criminal population. He laughed inwardly at the reminder of the nickname. Courtesy of Ben Hayes, now deceased.

Doc Woodruff sat down in the chair across from Dent, removed his glasses, and rubbed his eyes. "I'm sorry. Ben was a good man. I can hardly believe he's gone." He slipped the glasses back on, then scratched the silvery beard at his jaw. "The whole town will miss him, but his death sure leaves us with a problem. We've got no law here now. Word gets out—"

"Can't help ya. I've still got a prisoner to deliver to Cheyenne."

"Lock him up and wire for another deputy to do it."

Dent chafed at the suggestion. He always finished the job. But he had surely made a mess of this one. How in the heck had Needles grabbed his gun? One pretty face...one instant of distraction...then eternity for Ben, which made finishing this job all the more vital. "You know I can't do that."

Doc pursed his lips, as if the objection proved a point. "Dent, maybe it isn't my place to say this, but you're not exactly winning any prizes for the way you handle your duties. Sometimes, it's a nice surprise to hear you've delivered prisoners who are still upright in the saddle 'stead of slung across it."

"I never shot or killed anybody that wasn't tryin' to kill me. I don't start trouble, but I finish it."

Doc frowned at him, raising an eyebrow in a that's-not-the-whole-truth-and-you-know-it look. "I'm just saying maybe you could stand to relax a bit. I treated veterans after the war like you—the ones who had seen a lot of fighting. You're too ready to kill, Dent. Specializing in dying is no way to live."

Dent readied all kinds of justifications for what he did, but Ben's words came back to him. *One day you'll wake up fat, old, and alone—like me—and wonder what it was all for.*

"Anyway, my point is," Doc continued, "taking over for Ben for a while might show the folks in Evergreen and elsewhere you're not such a hothead. That you can cool down and back off when need be. And I think it would be good for *you* to quit hunting men for a while."

To Dent, staying in Evergreen for any reason sounded like a punishment akin to working a chain gang. Only a chain gang would be more exciting. He did owe Ben something, though, and most likely, there were some pretty ruffled feathers after this fiasco. His negligence had cost the town a good man and a fine sheriff. Dent didn't have a clue how he was ever gonna get past that, but sitting around watching mud dry didn't sound like the way to do it.

Doc slapped his knees and stood, Dent with him. "You think on that. And, while you're thinkin', you might want to pop your head inside my examination room and apologize to the lady whose head you fired at."

"I didn't fire at *her* head."

"She doesn't know that. For all she knows, you could've missed Needles." He tossed up a hand. "I know, I know, you don't miss. But it would be a nice gesture on your part to apologize to the girl. Heck of a welcome for our new schoolteacher. I'm not sure she'll stay now. She's pretty rattled by the reception." Doc winced at Dent's shirt. "And all that blood isn't gonna help. Why don't you change first? I've got a spare I'll loan you."

Dent sighed, a deep, weary exhalation of grief and frustration. "Sure."

~

Alone, sitting on the bed in the examination room, Amy stared at her hands. Would they ever quit shaking? Echoes of the gunfire resounded in her head. She plastered her palms over her ears in a futile effort to stop the noise.

She could still feel that vile man holding his hand against her stomach, his hot, sweaty body pressed to hers, and the cold point of the gun barrel between her breasts.

Somehow, it all blurred together with the attack back in Swanton. The acid taste of fear in her mouth, the men grabbing at her and spinning her around, the sound of her dress tearing, and the stench of cheap whiskey and filth filling her nostrils.

Her hand crept around to the back of her head as she recalled the pain of her skull smacking the sidewalk. It all still felt so real, as real as if she was back there again, screaming, clawing, the cold air swarming her shoulder as her dress was ripped away, that chilling laughter...and the single pistol shot that chased the attackers away.

She covered her face with her trembling, fragile hands and stifled the sobs crying for freedom. Slow, determined tears spilled down her cheeks. *Oh, God, why has all this happened? I feel like a shell of who I was. I'm so afraid...*

"Uh, ma'am?" a male voice called through the door as he knocked gently.

Amy wiped her face and squared her shoulders, but she didn't have the energy to stand. "Yes? Come in."

A handsome young man with shoulder-length, wavy, black hair and eyes the color of chocolate drops peered around the door. The marshal who had shot at her...or, rather, at her *assailant*. His square, handsome face, full of trepidation, warmed a bit, and he nodded as he stepped into the room. "I'm US Marshal Robert Hernandez. I wanted..." He trailed off and shrugged. "Um, I guess, to apologize. I'm sorry for all this trouble. I hope you're all right."

Amy stared at him, clueless as to a response. She didn't feel all right, not at all. "You could have shot me," slipped out. It felt good to let a little of the fear mix with some anger, and she rose. "What if you'd missed? Did you really think the place for a shoot-out was a crowded train platform? What kind of town is this?" Hysteria tried creeping into her voice. "I came here because I was assured Evergreen was a safe, quiet community with virtually no crime, and yet, I'm thrust in the middle of gunplay before I even step off the train."

"Ma'am," Dent patted the air and spoke gently. "I am truly sorry for what transpired. I'm truly sorry you were caught in the middle. However, I can assure you what happened today probably won't happen again in Evergreen for another hundred years."

Amy sank suddenly to the bed, her knees going all weak and wobbly. Peace and quiet. Crickets. Law-abiding residents. More churches than saloons. Her physician had assured her that Evergreen was the perfect place to quiet her fears and calm her nerves. She closed her eyes and tried slowing her racing heart. She despised this feeling of being so...emotionally precarious. "I was told there was no crime here. Not even petty larceny. Is that true, Deputy Hernandez?" She lifted her gaze to him and was surprised to find him staring back with a mixture of concern and confusion.

"I give you my word, miss, Evergreen is one of the

finest, safest towns in the West. You couldn't be any safer if you were back East."

She bit back a bitter laugh. "The East certainly isn't what it used to be...but I thank you for your assurance." She scanned the spartan little room and realized none of her belongings had come with her. Attempting to pull herself together, she stood once more and faced the marshal. "My things. My suitcases, satchel—"

Marshal Hernandez opened the door all the way and motioned to the outer room. "I'm sure between Doc and me, we can find your items and get you settled...um, wherever you'll be staying." Amy nodded a quick thank-you and moved to exit the room. As she passed by the marshal, he leaned in a little. "And one other thing, miss."

She paused, waiting.

"I wouldn't have shot you by accident. I never miss."

CHAPTER 3

"I'll take care of the bags, dear." Doc closed his office door behind the plump Mrs. Woodruff and the much more petite Miss Tate. Through the window, Dent absently watched the ladies amble down the boardwalk. His mind was back at the jail, wondering when he could head out with Happy.

Grinning, Doc tagged Dent in the ribs. "Yep, I guess I'd stare, too, if I was a young, single man."

Dent didn't catch Doc's drift at first, but then he shook his head. "No, sorry. I was lookin' in her direction, but thinking about Happy Jack. I need to go check on him and get my report written."

Doc reached up and laid the back of his hand on Dent's forehead, then touched the pulse at his neck. Flustered, Dent swatted his hand away. "What's the matter with you? I ain't sick."

Doc dropped his hand onto his hip. "I'm trying to make sure you're not *dead*. You even notice how pretty that gal is?"

Dent let his gaze drift out the window again. "Maybe." Which was the same thing as saying *not really.* "I've had a few things on my mind in the last hour."

"True." Doc sighed at the reminder of Ben's death, tugged his hat from a hook, and grabbed the doorknob. "Well, she's my houseguest till her cabin's ready. You come by for dinner. Maybe you'll take a minute to notice." He pulled the door open.

"I noticed her on the train, and now Ben's dead."

Doc stopped in his tracks. He thought for a moment, then wheeled around to Dent. Sixty or so, he was still tall and straight, and carried himself with authority. "It's not that girl's fault."

Dent flinched at the steel in his friend's tone. "No, sir. I didn't mean to imply it was."

The apology seemed to satisfy Doc. He nodded and slipped through the door. Dent was a little surprised by the man's unusual *protectiveness* of the new schoolteacher, but didn't give it much heed. His own misery and guilt crowded out the observation as he dropped his hat onto his head.

"A deal? You want to make a deal?" Dent looked past a wide-eyed, hopeful Happy Jack to the bars in the cell's window. He thought about all the times he'd passed through Evergreen on his way to find some outlaws. Ben had been a solid reminder that good men, law-abiding men, still held sway in the country. Now, he was gone and Dent had a good mad on. He was as surly as a bear. "No, Jack, I ain't too interested in a deal."

"Aw, come on, Marshal." Jack approached the bars. "I didn't know what Needles was gonna do, and I didn't help him. I stepped outta the way. That oughta be worth somethin'."

"Not really."

Jack scowled at Dent's deadpan answer. Then an evil tease lifted his brow. "What if I had some information?"

Dent sniffed and rested his hand on his gun. "For instance?"

The criminal grinned, showing a mouth full of rotten or missing teeth, and clutched the bars. "I hear tell every time you arrest somebody, you ask 'em a question."

"Which is?"

"Somethin' about 'was you in Sheridan on July 10, '67?'"

"Were you in *Evergreen*, on or about the evening of July *3*, 1880?"

"Yea, that's it." Jack squinted. "Why that date?"

"You said somethin' about some information."

Jack hesitated for a moment. "What if it *is* worth somethin' to ya?"

"I might mention to the territorial judge how you were not involved in the fray at the depot, and that you did not aid Needles in his attempt to escape…but I wouldn't bet on it."

Jack thought about it long and hard, then shrugged, as if he didn't have anything to lose. "I was in Fort Carson a few months ago. Played poker with a fella that said he shot a Wyoming lawman and probably would never step foot in the territory again. The lawman had a son who wouldn't let it go."

Dent had to admit the piece of information was intriguing, though specifics would have been helpful.

When and where in Wyoming had this supposed murder taken place? On its own, another useless clue. But the part about the lawman's son piqued his interest. "He didn't say a name? His or the lawman's? Can you describe this fella?"

"I did not get his name, or any others, but he wore a stovepipe hat and had bad scars on his wrists, like he'd been—"

"Shackled? Like he'd been on a chain gang?"

Jack smiled, big and wide. "Now that's information you can use."

Possibly. Identifying marks were usually mentioned on wanted posters, and the scarred wrists could mean the man had been on a railroad chain gang. "Fort Carson, huh?" Yes, these were solid leads. "I'll be sure the judge knows what happened today, Jack."

CHAPTER 4

Ben had saved all the wanted posters that came into his office. He had a collection going back twenty years. Dent pulled open the top drawer of the filing cabinet and scooped up an armful. If it took till the Second Coming, he would go through every one of these.

The second step, he'd take care of on the way to Doc's house. He'd send a telegram to the Union Pacific asking for the names of the prisons that had supplied chain gangs between the peak building years of '65 to '70. A shot in the dark, but maybe he'd get lucky and match some names with these wanted posters.

He dropped into the squeaking, leather office chair at the desk…and froze. How many times had Ben settled his old bones into this very seat and recalled his days chasing outlaws with Pa? Dent had loved those stories about the wild-and-woolly pair of lawmen.

Now, both of them were gone.

And Dent felt…lost.

He rubbed his temples and tried to think about business. The report he'd have to write…explaining how he'd let a killer get hold of his gun. Most likely, the report would end his career, and maybe that was as it should be. Penance.

Sagging inside, he leaned back in the chair and stared at the ceiling. *No way to fix this mess.*

Then plow right through it.

Working was better than wallowing in self-pity and grief. Determined not to waste a potential lead, he started flipping through the posters. The report, though, haunted his mind, poked at him like a kid with a stick. He couldn't sugarcoat a dang thing. Nothing he could do, in fact, except spell it out.

He shook his head and stood. If he had to write the report that would end his career, he could at least do it with a good dinner in him. He wouldn't shirk it. He'd write it tonight while it was still fresh in his mind, then turn it in tomorrow when he delivered Happy…

And let the chips fall where they may.

"Dent, I hate to talk about this at dinner," Doc ladled steaming chicken and dumplings onto his plate, the aroma filling the small dining room. "And I especially hate to talk about this in front of Miss Tate"—he nodded at the schoolmarm—"but, well, you're the only thing Ben's got for family. Least ways no one's seen his wife and son in years." He returned the spoon to the pot and settled back. "We need to make arrangements, and I know for a fact he left you his ranch—"

"His ranch?" Dent nearly choked on a dumpling. "He left me his ranch?"

"Oh, I know it doesn't really qualify as a ranch, what without cattle and all, but it's a fine spread. You could fix it up and—"

"No, no, no," Dent waved his hand, earning him a confused, almost fearful, look from Miss Tate. "I can't be tied down to property."

Dent's emphatic reaction brought the table to a halt. Susan Woodruff frowned hard and clutched the schoolteacher's hand, as if to assure her the US Marshal wasn't coming unglued. "Dent, no need to get so excited," she said gently. "If you don't want the property, you can always sell it, like you did your pa's place. The more immediate need would be to talk to Pastor Wills to arrange Ben's funeral."

Dent sighed so heavily he about blew the food off the table. He wasn't prepared for any of this. Dang, he wished he could shoot Needles again, just to make himself feel better. "Susan, I'm between a rock and a hard place." He rubbed his jaw and shifted his attention to Doc. "I've got that business tomorrow over in Cheyenne."

Doc's eyes narrowed and he and Susan swapped strained glances. Unspoken messages swirled at the table. Perhaps aware there was something here that was none of her business, Miss Tate dropped her head as if her vittles had suddenly become more interesting.

"Yes, that business," Doc repeated. "Not something you can get out of, at least not at this late date."

"Henry and I can talk to the pastor," Susan offered. "We'll make the arrangements, if that's all right with you."

"That's best, Susan, if you don't mind. Thank you." And Dent truly was appreciative. The feeling that he was drowning rose up in him. Given the choice, he preferred a hanging to making funeral arrangements and wondered what that said about the condition of his heart.

Specializing in dyin'...

"Miss Tate," Susan shifted her attention to their guest, "this *can* wait until after supper," she flicked a warning glance at Doc. "Let's talk about something more pleasant. You." She patted the girl's hand. "I understand you were a librarian most recently, but you have been a schoolteacher?"

Dismissed from the conversation, and glad of it, Dent hunkered down over his food and focused on eating.

"Yes, ma'am." The girl laid her fork down and shoved her glasses up a bit. "I taught elementary school for six years, but I love books so much that when I had the opportunity to move to the library, I jumped at it."

Dent stabbed a dumpling and almost laughed at the girl's history. Since she was about as exciting as a brick, he figured she'd fit right in with Evergreen. A schoolmarm *and* a librarian. At least he'd never be arresting her for anything. And maybe he *had* noticed she was a little on the pretty side. He risked a quick glance to confirm that. Her cheeks were soft and smooth, flawless, and the color of a ripe peach. Dainty auburn curls wafted gently around her face as she moved. Dent ducked back to the safety of his meal.

Doc pushed a biscuit around his plate as he sopped up the remaining chicken broth. "In case you were wondering, Miss Tate, the town doesn't know much about your personal history."

An odd, stilted tone in the man's voice drew Dent back in. He saw the cautious exchange between Miss Tate and her hosts. Something had been said without being said, but he couldn't have cared less. He had his own matters to worry about.

Susan picked up the pitcher and poured more water for herself and Miss Tate. "The search committee tells me you will be starting a library as well as teaching?" Dent heard the forced cheer, getting them past the unspoken message.

"Yes, ma'am." Miss Tate wiped her mouth and set her napkin on the table. "Because of my work at the library, I've met many, many patrons who love to share the joy of reading. I'm sure we'll have hundreds of books donated by spring."

"Oh, that's so exciting. I love to read, too." Susan rose and started to clear the table. "Well, we'll have dessert and coffee in the living room."

"Let me help," Miss Tate started to rise.

"No, no," Susan shook her head. "You're a guest. You and Dent go on in." She waved a hand toward the hallway. "Henry and I will bring in the pie." Susan pulled Dent's plate away from him, although he wasn't done. He followed it stubbornly for a moment, but her raised brow convinced him to let it go. Not sure why she was in such a hurry to get him away from the table, he licked his fork, and surrendered it. "Fine. I'll stoke the fire." He rose and left the room.

Amy could have huffed her indignation at the marshal's abrupt departure from the room, but clearly, he would not have noticed. He seemed *totally* absorbed in his own matters.

"He was raised better, Miss Tate," Dr. Woodruff rose and proceeded to assist his wife by picking up his own plate and glass. "I hope you'll overlook his preoccupation. It's been a difficult day for him...for everyone."

"Ben was probably his oldest friend." Susan hoisted a stack of dirty dishes to her hip and hooked two mugs with her fingers. "And...he's never dealt well with grief."

Considering the circumstances, Amy should have let it go. Not being escorted from the dinner table by a gentleman was certainly not the worst thing that had ever happened to her. No, it was more than that. The marshal looked right through her, as if she wasn't even in the room. She'd been through quite a bit lately, but still had some pride. Being treated as if she were no more important than a rug on the floor stung.

Susan backed up to the kitchen door, her arms full of dishes. "Go on, now. We'll be right there with the pie and coffee."

Amy nodded at her and Doc and slipped across the hallway to the parlor. She found the marshal kneeling at the fire, his hand resting on the poker, his thoughts somewhere far away. She hesitated about interrupting his reverie and took the moment to study him. Obviously not yet thirty, weathered lines fringed the corners of his eyes, giving him an air of wisdom and experience men back East didn't possess. His brooding reminded her of Emily Brontë's Heathcliff. She would admit, though, there was something *comforting* about him. She attributed this feeling to his badge.

That night intruded on her thoughts again, threatened to start her heart racing, and she knew it would be a long, long time before she ever let a man near her again...even a lawman. She pushed the hopelessness of the future away and laced her fingers over her stomach, quelling the queasy feeling trying to rise in her. After a moment, he still hadn't noticed her standing there. A little frustrated, she stepped quietly into the room, allowing the swish of her skirt to announce her. He rose to greet her...and said absolutely nothing.

The awkward moment stretching on to ridiculous lengths, Amy finally thought of something to rescue them. "I'm sorry for your loss. I understand the sheriff was a friend."

"Yes, ma'am. Thank you."

The silence fell again. The marshal shoved his hands into his pockets and smiled weakly. She had seen men who were socially inept and men who were disinterested in conversation. Amy realized he gave *disinterested* a new meaning. Breaking eye contact as a mercy to him, she dipped her head, smiled, and strode over to the settee. Taking a seat, she sighed inwardly. As a houseguest, she certainly couldn't pick and choose the Woodruffs' company. And she supposed she should be grateful the marshal wasn't a chatting magpie.

But neither was he pleasant. Oh, she knew she should make allowances for his circumstances, but his brusqueness was annoying. And frankly, rude. She hoped to avoid him as much as possible in the future.

ABOUT THE AUTHOR

Heather Blanton is a *USA Today* bestselling author of thirty Christian Western romances, including the highly rated and awarded Romance in the Rockies series. She is also an award-winning script writer. Her Romance in the Rockies series has been optioned for a limited TV series, and her script *Unbridled Hearts* is currently optioned as well.

She grew up in the mountains of Western North Carolina on a steady diet of *Bonanza, Gunsmoke,* and John Wayne Westerns. Her daddy taught her to shoot when she was five, and she can hit that at which she aims.

Her novels are all Christian Western romance because she enjoys creating feisty pioneer women who struggle to find love and hold on to their faith. Like all good, old-fashioned Westerns, there is always justice, a moral message, American values, lots of high adventure, unexpected plot twists, and often a touch of suspense.

www.authorheatherblanton.com

www.ingramcontent.com/pod-product-compliance
Lightning Source LLC
LaVergne TN
LVHW040220110826
845146LV00005B/1353

* 9 7 9 8 8 9 5 6 7 8 5 4 1 *